FATE IS N

By: Pete Botto Jr.

Copyright: TXu2-133-867

DEDICATION

God gave us two things: Fate and Free Will. Fate is his gift to us; a gift that will find us no matter how lost in the chaos we become. Free Will consists of our gift back to God; it provides endless opportunities to show God how much we appreciate what He gave to us. This book is dedicated to those who may have been beaten and battered by the happenings of everyday life, but never lost sight of the anchor that is Faith.

A very special Thank You goes out to Alex Evans. Ironically, yours was a voice that electronically reached out to me when I needed it the most. Your thoughts, opinions and naturally caring nature means more to me than I can express.

Copyright: TXu2-133-867

CHAPTER LIST

FATE IS NEVER LATE

CHAPTER ONE

I always pictured my death vividly. I would be an old man, perhaps eighty-six years old. I would be lying on my own bed, in my own home. My wife and children surrounding me (not like on the bed with me like in Willy Wonka, that would be creepy, but sitting in chairs in the room). Their presence would give me peace as I prepared myself to face whatever came next. I was not scared to die; I believe in God and Heaven. That is not to say that I would not miss this life, but I took comfort in knowing I could look over my children and continue to watch them grow.

That all changed the day I received "the call". My wife was out celebrating the promotion of her co-worker, Maria, at a bar near their office; I was home with the kids. Donovan was on his cell phone talking with his friends; they would do a conference call while watching the same television show. Considering they all lived within three miles of each other, I never understood why they did not just meet at the house and watch it together. However, times had changed since I was seventeen, so who was I to question it?

My other son, Devin, was working on a science project. Or, I guess I should say, I was working on his science project. "We" had to create a model of a plant cell using a Styrofoam ball. I was in the process of digging through the pantry to find a cheese-ball to use as the nucleus when I heard the house phone ring. Since only solicitors and telemarketers call the landline, I ignored it. A moment later, it rang again.

Frustrated, because the damn cheese ball would break every time I stuck a toothpick in it, I yelled out to my youngest, "Destiny, will you please answer that?"

With all the teenage angst she could muster, she blew her hair out of her face and answered the call. "Dad, it's for you.", she yelled, even though I was ten feet away from her.

"No shit, Sherlock.", I replied, "Who is it?" She asked who it was and then turned to me with a concerned look.

"He says he is with the Hillsborough County Sherriff's office.", she said, reaching out the phone to me.

"I just donated to their golf tournament.", I said, somewhat annoyed, "What do they want now?", I asked, more to the air than to Destiny.

She rolled her eyes. "They want to talk to you."

I brought my fist down, crushing what was left of the cheese-ball. "Fine.", I whined, walking over to retrieve the phone.

"Hello.", I said, looking back at the orange dust I would now need to clean from the table.

"Mr. Moretti?", the voice asked.

"Yes, this is Mr. Moretti.", I replied, wondering if it would be easier just to paint the rest of the table orange.

"This is Deputy Alcover from the Hillsborough County Sherriff's office. Is Sara Moretti your wife?"

"Did she finally get caught sneaking rolls into her purse? If so, I do not know her.", I said.

"No sir. There has been an accident. She is at Tampa General Hospital."

It's funny how ten words can make you forget how to speak. "Is...is she okay?", I finally stammered.

"You may want to get there as soon as you can.", he said, solemnly.

I don't know if I even hung up the phone. I threw the handset onto the couch, ran to the kitchen, pulled my keys off the wall holder, and made a beeline for the front door. "Donovan, watch your brother and sister!", I yelled, as I slammed the door behind me. Hell, for all I know, I left the door open; all that consumed my mind was, "There has been an accident."

FATE IS NEVER LATE

When I pulled up at the hospital, I had no idea how I had gotten there. I recall my cell phone ringing a couple times, but it was the kids and I was not ready to tell them what had happened yet. I pulled into the first empty parking space; it was a handicap space, but fuck it, they could tow me. I ran up to the nurse's station and told her my wife had been in an accident. I know they hear this day-in-and-day-out, but it still amazed me how calm the nurse could be.

After giving her my wife's name, she checked the computer then asked me to sit in the family waiting room. "No offense, ma'am, but I need to see my wife NOW!", I demanded. I couldn't make out the expression on her face; either she was doing to her best to remain cordial (I would not have blamed her for coming back at me) or she was felt sorry me (which drove me crazy because I didn't know if she felt sorry because my wife was in an accident or because I was taking it out on her).

"Sir, I must ask you to wait there. I promise, someone will be with you shortly." All I could think about was my wife lying somewhere alone, broken and battered. The waiting room was directly across from the nurse's station. I took a seat in the first empty chair, but I turned to face the nurse. I wanted to make sure she was calling someone to let them know I was there. She looked up at me, as she whispered into the phone, which I took as reassurance that she was sending someone to take me to Sara.

Finally, after what felt like hours but was probably just minutes, a doctor walked up to me. "Mr. Moretti?", he asked.

I leapt to my feet. "Yes. How is my wife?", I asked.

"Please come with me.", he said.

As we walked, I expected him to stop at every drawn curtain and pull it back to reveal Sara. I had a mixture of fear and relief as we passed each curtain and it was left in place.

Finally, we came to what looked like a small, empty office. "In here, please.", he said.

"Wait..what? I want to see Sara.", I replied, somewhere between a whisper and a shout.

"Mr. Moretti, please come in. I will let you know what is going on."

Reluctantly, I followed him into the room. The room was as I suspected; it was the size of a glorified closet. The only furnishings were two green, padded chairs with a small table in-between them.

"Mr. Moretti.", he began.

"Ray, please call me Ray."

"Ray….your wife was in a very serious accident."

I already knew this! Why did he think I was at the hospital? I needed to know how she was. "Doctor, I know. How is she?", I begged to know.

"I am afraid, when the paramedics arrived on the scene, your wife was already gone."

FATE IS NEVER LATE

"Gone? Gone where?", I asked, either not grasping what he was telling me or not wanting to.

"She had already passed away, Mr. Mor...Ray. I am very sorry for your loss." He went to place his hand on my shoulder, but I jerked away from his touch. I stood. "She can't be dead!", I shouted, "When the officer called, he said she was taken here." The doctor reached out to me again, but pulled his hand back before he made contact.

"All victims are brought here, regardless of their condition. They must be....pronounced.", he said.

"Victim? Victim? She is not a victim. She is a wife...and a mother! She cannot be dead!", I shouted.

"Ray, I am very sorry, but she was dead upon their arrival. There was nothing that could be done for her."

My knees gave way and I collapsed into the chair. "Would you like some water?", he asked.

"No! I would like to wake up now!"

FATE IS NEVER LATE

"Again, I am very sorry. If you would like to take a few minutes; I can then take you to her body."

The room was spinning. Her body? What about her soul? What about her brown eyes that slanted along with her smile? What about her ears that would turn red at the tips every time she laughed? What about her voice; the faint melody it carried even when she was upset or angry? What about all those things? That is what I wanted to see and to hear!

I stood up and walked out of the room. "Mr. Moretti.", the doctor called after me, "Where are you going?"

I didn't look back. "I am leaving."

"Sir, we need you to identify her body." He almost had to shout as I was halfway down the hall.

"I am not going to see my wife that way. I am going to go home to be with my kids. If Sara does not walk through the door, I will know 'the body' you say you have belongs to her."

"Sir, arrangements need to be made.", I heard him say as I pushed open the door and headed to my car. As I slammed the car door closed, my world came crashing down. I tried to rest my head on the steering wheel, but my body was shaking too badly. I pulled on the lever and let my body fall back with the seat. I covered my face with my hands, as even the light from the outside bulb was too much of an intrusion.

She couldn't be dead. She was supposed to walk through the door, telling Donovan to get off the phone before the door was closed behind her. She would then come up to the table, give me that 'shouldn't Devin be doing that' look as she kissed me on the forehead. She would then hang her purse on the arm of the chair as she grabbed a handful of the remaining cheeseballs. She would then go sit on the couch next to Destiny and pull her close. She would take a few minutes to unwind and we would then sit down to the table for dinner.

What would I tell the kids? How could I tell the kids? How do you speak the words that will shatter their lives forever? How do you tell them that their mother will never come in their room, after they are supposed to be asleep, to make sure they are tucked in? How do you tell them that they will never see her standing at the stove in her 'Tacos? That is what I thought!' apron, singing along to Aretha as she browned the ground beef? How do you tell them that when they look up from the graduation platform, they will see only an empty seat beside me, where she is supposed to be? How do you tell them that there will never be a mother-of-the-groom or of the bride? How do you tell them that their children will never have their grandmother there to spoil them?

I picked up my phone and the bile rose in my throat upon seeing my screensaver, which was the five of us at Disneyworld; all of us smiling with our arms around each other. I picked up my phone again but made it a point to only look at the phone icon at the bottom. I had eight missed calls and twelve text messages.

FATE IS NEVER LATE

God help me, but I couldn't do this alone. "You better get used to doing things alone.", my mind whispered to me. My vision blurred and my fingers fumbled as I tried to touch the phone icon, so I had to give Siri the request to make the call for me.

When Sara's sister, Michelle, picked up the phone, I couldn't speak. I opened my mouth, but only sobs poured forth.

"Ray? Ray? Are you okay?", I heard her asking.

"It….it is Sara.", I finally managed to say, "Michelle, she is gone." I could not bring myself to say the word dead.

"Where are you asked?", in a panic.

I could not get any more words out. I hit 'send location' and hung up. The rational part of my brain was trying to scream that doing that was wrong; however, the majority of me was too far gone to give it a second thought.

At some point, there came a knock at my window. I looked up to see Michelle's tear-stained face looking down at me. I leaned up and pulled on the handle to open the door.

"Ray.", she said reaching down to me, "What happened?"

I couldn't speak. I put my hands over my face in reply. I could not bear to look at her.

"Wait here with him. I will go in and find out what is going on.", Michelle's husband, Tim, told her.

Michelle knelt and took ahold of my hands. "Ray, please. Tell me what happened."

I looked at Michelle, but I could not see her through my tears. "She was in an accident. They said she did not make it.", I choked out.

Michelle wrapped her arms around me and together we cried. "Where are the kids?", she finally asked.

"They are at home. They do not know. I cannot tell them."

"Let me go check on Tim and we will figure this out."

Before she made it to the door, Tim walked out, a solemn look on his face. He shook his head and Michelle fell into his arms. "Let my heart give out, Lord.", I thought, "I have to be with her." That is when my phone rang again, snapping me out of the dark thoughts. The kids. I was all they had left and they were my world. They would need me now, more than ever. I hit 'decline', but immediately texted that I would be home soon. I hoped that would be enough for now.

"Come on.", Michelle said, "Get in our car. Tim is going to take us to your house."

My house. The words reached in and squeezed what was left of my heart. It was our house. It would always be our house. I laid in the back seat and closed my eyes. I prayed the ride would be a long one; of course, in no time at all, we arrived at the house.

I am sorry, but the pain is still too intense to describe how we told the children and their reactions. I am sure you can imagine without my describing it to you. That was, and will always be, the worst moment of my life. I thought the kids finding out that Santa was not real was the worst heartache I would ever have to see them endure; I was wrong….very,very wrong!

CHAPTER TWO

It had been a year since I dropped Donovan off at the campus of Florida State University. It was two years since Sara had passed. I was now dropping off Devin who would room with his older brother. Destiny and I both sat in the car and cried after Devin was safely in his room.

To say the last two years had been difficult would be an understatement. However, with her brothers now away at college, I worried that I would not be enough for Destiny. She was always very close to her brothers, but even more so after Sara passed. She was always 'Daddy's girl', but would I be enough?

"One more year and you will be here with them.", I told her, hoping that would ease some of her pain.

"Are you trying to get rid of me already?", she asked, jokingly.

The familiar pain gripped my heart. "You are lucky if I let you go. I have already purchased the handcuffs and duct tape just to be safe."

"You know I can go to Hillsborough Community College instead.", she said, with absolute sincerity.

"Baby Girl, you have an amazing life and endless opportunities ahead of you. As much as I would like to keep you home with me forever, it would be so much less than you deserve. Your mother would haunt me until the end of my days.", I tried to laugh, but it caught in my throat.

"You have to put yourself back out there dad.", she said, "No one can ever replace mom, but I cannot leave knowing you are alone. You talk about what I deserve, but what about you?"

FATE IS NEVER LATE

I waved off her comment. "You kids are all I need.", I assured her.

She took my hand. "Seriously, dad. Donovan and Devin are already out of the house and, like you said, I am only a year away myself. Even before mom passed, you have dedicated every moment of your life to us; you have to think about yourself too."

I looked straight into her beautiful brown eyes; so much like her mother's. "Destiny, you kids are my life and all I have ever wanted. Every moment I spend with the three of you has always been the greatest moment of my life. I have never wanted for anything more.", I assured her.

"Exactly my point.", she replied, "What are you going to do next year? Are you going to stare at the ceiling waiting for us to come home on our breaks? What kind of life is that? I don't think I have ever seen you go out to do something

FATE IS NEVER LATE

for yourself. You need to get out there. The thought of leaving you alone kills me.", she said. It killed me too.

"I will cross that bridge when I get to it.", I told her. "Right now, I still have you and I intend to make the most of every second for the next year."

She hugged me and kissed my cheek. "As much as I look forward to that, and I really do, I am not going to give up on you getting you to do more for yourself.", she warned. She held true to her threat.

Destiny did not give me too much grief for a couple months. However, about five months before she was set to leave for college, she devised a plan to 'get me out there'.

"Tinder? What is Tinder?", I asked, looking down at my phone.

"It is a social site, dad.", she told me. "You mean a dating site.", I shot back.

"It can be used for dating, but it is good for meeting like-minded people.", she said.

"So, it specializes in introverts who have no interest in dating?", I asked, sarcastically.

"It has everything.", she said, grabbing the phone from my hand. "Look.", she said, opening the app and choosing the 'settings' option. "You can enter as little or as much information about yourself as you like. Then, on the next page, you enter what type of person you would be a good match for. Tinder does the rest."

"Destiny, your mother is the only woman I will ever love.", I told her. "Dad, I know that. I told you, this is not only a dating site. You can meet some people. Go out and have a couple drinks, play pool, go bowling, climb Mount Everest...anything you want to do.", she replied.

FATE IS NEVER LATE

"Wow! I was just thinking, the other day, that I wanted to climb Mount Everest, but I didn't want to do it alone."

She rolled her eyes. "I'm serious, dad!"

"Destiny, I am serious too. In many ways. Like when I tell you that your mother is the only woman I will ever love."

She looked at me with understanding that she should not have. "Then find yourself a man.", she said, "The option for that is right here.", she said, going to the 'looking for' section of the app.

"What do you mean by that?", I asked her, curiously.

"Dad, do you really think we do not know that you dated men before you fell in love with mom? You know that Aunt Lynn cannot keep anything a secret."

My damn sister! I was going to kill her! "And that did not bother you?", I asked her, unwilling to believe that it would not.

"Hello, dad. Welcome to 2018.", she said, "It doesn't matter who you loved before mom or after mom. We always knew that you loved mom with your all your heart and soul."

My head was spinning. I had not even thought of my life before Sara since the day I first laid eyes on her. I had no reason, nor desire, to. Sara was the only part of my past and future that ever mattered. A future that was stolen from us.

"And your brothers know too?", I asked her.

She rolled her eyes. "Seriously, dad. Have we ever been able to keep anything from each other? Anyway, Lynn told us when we were all together."

The anger in me rose again. Lynn was always the kind of person who was quick to share everyone's business but her own. "When was this?", I asked. "About six or seven years ago, I guess.", she replied.

"I can't believe you all have known that long."

"Like I said, it didn't matter then and it doesn't matter now.", she said, very matter-of-factly, "Maybe it would easier for you to hang out with another man."

I didn't want to think about having to meet anyone: man or woman. Destiny was still here for a couple of months and then the kids would still come home over breaks and on holidays. That was all I needed.

"Here.", she said, handing me my phone, "I put that you were a man looking for another man for friendship.

If you ever want to change that, you just go into the settings."

Reluctantly, I thanked her and put the phone on the coffee table. I didn't need Tinder; I needed a fun night out with my daughter. We went to eat at LaTeresita and then I took her to GameTime Arcade in Ybor City. After we diminished what was left of my money and my pride; we headed home.

"I am sleeping at Jennifer's tonight; if that is okay?", she asked.

"Of course it is, baby. Go and have fun...but not too much fun!", I warned. That earned me another eye roll. "I will call Jennifer and tell her to cancel the stripper.", she sighed.

"Girl, you thought I was kidding that time I told you I had handcuffs and duct tape? Don't make me use them.", I warned.

"Why don't you check out Tinder.", she said, "Maybe you will find a reason to use them after all."

She did it...she left me speechless.

It wasn't until I reached for my phone to text Destiny goodnight, that I remembered I had left it on the coffee table, downstairs. I didn't feel like going down to get it, but I would never be able to fall asleep until I texted her 'goodnight'.

When I picked up my phone, I saw the little "1" notification floating on top of the Tinder app, which Destiny had put on my home screen. I don't know why seeing that little "1" made me so nervous. It felt like a stranger was trying to invade my personal space.

I ignored the blaring notification and sent the text to Destiny. I placed my phone on the nightstand, turned off the light and buried my head in the pillow. A moment later, I heard an unfamiliar 'ding'. Worried that Destiny may be texting me from Jennifer's phone, I picked up the phone to check it. There was now a "2" displayed in the corner of the Tinder app.

"Damn you, Destiny.", I thought. I placed the phone back on the nightstand; however, even with my eyes closed, I could still see that taunting "2". I picked up the phone and hit the icon.

CHAPTER THREE

The first message was from the moderators at Tinder thanking me for joining. I would pass their thanks on to Destiny since she was the one who technically joined. The second was from a man that was, supposedly, four miles away.

The message read, "Sup. What you looking for?" Although true, I assumed "The damn remote.", was not the answer he was looking for. I was going to ignore the message, until a second message came in while I was reading the first.

"Hey man. You DTF?", he typed. Now remember, I have three teenagers; I know what DTF means. I quickly replied, "Nope".

"Then what are you looking for?"

"I'm not really looking for anything. My daughter signed me up for this.", I replied. The green light, which indicated he was currently online, quickly went red.

Seriously questioning what options Destiny chose, I pulled up the settings. As far as I could tell, she had only chosen the 'looking for friends' option. That guy must have thought I was very friendly.

I closed the app, finally found the remote and let Netflix recommend something I may like. Hopefully Netflix knew me a little bit better than that guy did. Netflix recommended Sense8. It sounded interesting, so I hit 'play'. Fifteen minutes into the first episode, I was hooked.

As I lay there contemplating how Darryl Hannah could actually be the mother to all of these people, I realized that was beside the point. I loved how all these people, who had never met each other, could somehow be connected. Besides my family, I had not felt connected to anyone in a long time. Maybe Destiny was right; maybe I had to put myself out there. I would consider it, but I knew Tinder was not the way to do it.

The next day, I googled, 'How to meet new people in my area'. There were hundreds of sites that came up; most of them appeared to be along the same lines as Tinder. I was not DTF, so I dismissed those. One of them caught my eye; it was called 'MeetUp'. From the description, you could join groups which contained members that shared similar interests. They had everything from 'Lets Bowl' to 'Naked Archery'. Hopefully the naked archers had one or two medical professionals as members.

It looked interesting, so I clicked the 'Join Now' button. It asked for my name and email address to sign up. I felt comfortable using my name, but I did not want my inbox inundated with spam, so I decided to create a separate email.

Thanks to the seemingly infinite availability provided by Gmail, my new email was ForFriendship33@gmail.com. DTF69@gmail was already taken. Just kidding! Feeling confident with my new email address, I signed up for MeetUp.

I could have spent all day going through all the groups the site offered. I was having a hard time deciding what groups I would even want to join. Sure, I loved to swim, but did I really want to join 'Let's Get Wet'? I love to swim, but I had a feeling these people LOOOOVE to swim. I passed on that one.

The first one that truly caught my interest was 'By the Book'. It was a book club-based group. Although I have never liked for others to dictate what I read, I do love to read. I could do this. It was reading and discussing what we read; how hard could that be?

Apparently 'By the Book' is somewhat exclusive. Before you are "approved", you must answer a couple questions first. The answers are then reviewed by the 'Master of Meetup' or some such person and then you are either deemed worthy or told to stick to the local library. I was a little put off by the fifth question, so when it asked, "Why would you be a good addition to this group?", I put, "Because I like to read books and discuss them and shit like that." Apparently, that was the correct answer; I was approved the same day.

There were twenty-six members of the group and eight of them were meeting tonight to discuss the ending of "Little Women" and voting on their next book. Although I had never read the book, I have heard enough about it to know that it is not about feminine midgets. I heard, at some point in my life, that the author loosely based the story on the lives or her and her three sisters. That always interested me. I would bet that many books are loosely based on the lives of the author.

I debated showing up late, since I would not have anything to contribute to the first part of the get together, but I didn't want to be rude on my first meet-up. In fact, as usual, I showed up before everyone else. One of my biggest pet peeves are people who show up late all the time. That and people who don't use their blinker. You paid for it- use it!

When I arrived, the host, Carol, welcomed me. She asked me if I had read the book. I admitted I had not. She assured me that would not hamper the event, as long as I did not mind hearing how the book ends. Doubting I would ever be inclined to read it, I had no problem with that.

The meet-up went very well. I was the only man there, which was a little uncomfortable at first, but all the members made me feel welcome.

Although, I now knew the ending of the book, I will admit it sounded interesting. It is not that I had anything against the book; my interest tends to veer more towards anything with vampires, werewolves or angels in it. Having said that, I suggested the book 'Gris Gris' for the groups next read. I assured them that it was not your typical vampire novel. I have read the book numerous times, but it is the type of book you can read over and over without growing tired of it.

On my way home, I called Destiny to thank her for encouraging me to get back out there. I thought there was a problem with the connection when she asked, "Who is this?" It took me a minute to realize she was just being a smartass.

Of course, she asked if there were any good-looking women or men in the group, to which I answered by disconnecting the call. That girl is so lucky I love her so much.

Since the first event went so well, I searched for other groups that night. This time, 'Introverted Extroverts' jumped out at me. It was a group for people who were, by nature, introverted, but longed to release their inner extrovert. I could not image ever being considered an extrovert, but Destiny would approve of the group.

I signed up, thankful that I only had to answer two admittance questions this time. They were, "Are you an introvert or extrovert?" and "If you are an introvert, will you really show up to any events?" The second question made me laugh. Even as I was signing up, I was thinking, "I am never going to go to any of their events."

The size of this group was a little more intimidating. They had over 100 members. I scanned the upcoming events and chose the one that just enough participants to not be overwhelming, but enough to where I would not have to interact if I chose not to.

Hey, it is a group geared towards introverts, right? For all I knew, we all may spend the whole event awkwardly sitting in silence. The event was a card game, so at least we would have something to generate conversation or help us avoid it, depending on what the case may be.

I was not going to tell Destiny about this one, in case I decided not to go. There were twelve members that RSVP'd. The only time I interact with that many people is at work and that is only because I have to.

When Saturday rolled around, I threw caution to the wind and went to the event. I was relieved there were actually men at this one. Not that I have a problem with women. In fact, my best friends have always been women. My issue was how many of the women in the book club group were single. As soon as they found out I was a widow, their interests were peaked a little too much for my comfort. I had no intention of dating anyone- woman or man.

As I surveyed the crowd, everyone seemed fairly mellow. That is, until Vincent and Alan arrived. I quickly determined that Vincent was the introvert and Alan the extrovert. However, the whole yin and yang thing worked perfectly for them. During the night, I learned they were a couple. They recently moved from Seattle to Tampa and also figured MeetUp was the best way to meet new people.

I never realized how detached I was from the 'gay' lifestyle. The last time I had a boyfriend, I was sixteen years old. Back then, being gay was taboo. The only people it was safe to be yourself around were the rare few you met who were also gay. My boyfriend and I would never hold hands or show affection in public. Hell, one time we were almost stabbed after leaving a pool hall because two of the guys playing at the table next to us 'thought we were gay'.

We had done absolutely nothing to make anyone think we were a couple; they just assumed. Yes, they assumed correctly, but that is not the point. I knew, and was very glad, that gay rights had come a long way over the years; yet, my stomach immediately clenched when I saw Alan lean over and give Vincent a kiss. I quickly looked around the table, waiting for a snide comment or nasty look, but there was no change in anyone's expression. I was stunned; the others were not phased at all.

Much to my surprise, I exchanged phone numbers with Vincent and Alan before I left. They were both incredible guys and I really enjoyed meeting them. My head was still spinning over the acceptance of everyone in the group.

Mind you, even at sixteen (or maybe because I was sixteen), I never cared what anyone thought about me having a boyfriend. Yet, I knew how society viewed it and I knew it would not be an easy path. Fuck easy. I didn't need easy, I just needed to be happy.

From a very young age, I had always been attracted to men and women. To me, it was natural. I never had the inner debate as to which I would choose; I never looked at as a choice. It wasn't until much later in life that I heard the term 'bisexual'. At the time I heard it, it meant nothing to me. By that time, I had already fallen in love with Sara and married her.

I have been asked many times how I could have dated a man but fallen in love with a woman. I always reply, "Was it a conscious decision when you fell in love with your spouse, boyfriend, girlfriend, etc.?" No! The heart knows what the heart knows. My heart made it very clear that I was in love with Sara. It was not a choice; it was fate.

FATE IS NEVER LATE

Not too long ago, I heard the term 'pansexual'. To me, that term made so much more sense for my situation. It is not as cut and dry as being bisexual, which is being attracted to men and women. Pansexuality is being attracted to the qualities that someone possesses; regardless of what is camped out behind their zipper.

People have always made such a big deal about sexuality; even in this day and age it is still the way so many people are defined. I have never understood that. Why would someone's sexuality even be a topic or an issue? That is such a small part of who a person is (or at least it should be). I am more concerned whether you hold the door open for people than I am about who you are bumping uglies with.

What I realized tonight was that my mindset regarding homosexuality was stuck in the late 80's. The last time I had to even think about it, it was something that society wanted you to be ashamed of. It was something suspected, but rarely confirmed. In the 80's, you didn't have a boyfriend, you had a 'good friend' or a 'roommate'. I was very happy for Vincent and Alan that so much had changed.

CHAPTER FOUR

The time finally came for Destiny to join her brothers in college. I seriously considered driving right pass the school and taking her to Canada or something; anyplace she could not easily leave. Of course, I gave in and soon she was reunited with her brothers and I was alone.

The drive home was worse than I expected it to be. All I could think of was the cold, dark house that awaited me. I could not even think of it as a home; home was where my kids were.

As my exit approached, I did something I never thought I would do, I kept driving. I drove until I was in an area I had never been to before. I had no destination in mind; I only knew where I did not want to be.

About forty minutes into my detour, I saw a little hole-in-the-wall bar with the rainbow flag hanging outside. I pulled in. I sat there, in the car, just staring at the entrance. I don't even drink; what was I doing there?

I thought about calling Vincent and Alan to see what they were doing, but I recalled their earlier Facebook post stating they were at Disney for the day.

I had two choices, neither that I wanted to do: go inside or go home. I went inside. I had no idea what to expect. Would it be evident to those inside that I did not belong there? To say I felt like a fish out of the water would be a massive understatement.

I avoided looking at anyone and headed to the part of the bar where there were multiple empty chairs. When the bartender, a cute younger guy wearing an award-winning smile and a fishnet tank top, asked me what I wanted, I almost answered, "To be anywhere but here." Instead, I ordered a Corona Light.

The marketing representatives from Corona would be happy to know the signage they hung up in the bar generated a sale. The bartender asked if I wanted a lemon with that. Sure, a lemon....a bullet....whatever.

I was afraid to look around. I didn't want anyone to think that I was checking them out and I really did not want to talk to anyone. I just wanted to feel something besides sad; fear was an acceptable replacement.

I heard a commotion to my left, which pulled my attention from the worn wood on the bar. I should have just kept my head down! There was an older man, around sixty-five or so, stumbling my way. For every step forward he tried to take, he would veer sideways, almost knockin over every barstool in the process.

I knew I was the only person sitting in his trajectory, so I quickly turned my head, as to not draw attention. It didn't work. I felt a heavy arm drape over my shoulder. When I turned my head, his face was an inch from mine. Even that close, I could see the man was too far gone to even focus.

"Hey.", he slurred. I tried to back up as far as the barstool would allow, which was not far.

"Hello.", I reluctantly replied.

"Kandoduckyou?", is what I heard come out of his mouth.

"I'm sorry?", I said, praying that spittle did not fly out of his mouth and land on my face.

"Can I fuck you a little?", he asked, a little more slowly but just as slurred as before.

"Excuse me?", I asked, knowing I had to have heard wrong.

"Can I fuck you a little?", he asked again.

I extended my hand to get him out of my face. "Did you seriously just ask me if you could fuck me a little?", I asked.

"Yep. So, can I?", he slurred, trying to close the distance between us, oblivious to my arm being in the way.

"What the hell does that even mean? How do fuck someone a little?", I practically shouted.

I started to stand when I heard a voice say, "Albert, are you trying to make a move on my boyfriend?". I felt someone take Albert's arm from around my neck and they replaced it with their own. I turned to look at the source of the arm and was totally confused.

The owner of the arm was adorable. He had beautiful baby blue eyes and a smile that put the bartenders to shame. He winked at me and mouthed, "play along".

"Now, Albert, what have I told you? You cannot hit on every man that comes into the bar; especially my boyfriend."

"Awww, Jake.", the man said, pouting. "Go on.", Jake said, "Go back to your barstool."

As clumsily as Albert had arrived; he left. I wanted to make sure he was safely near his barstool before I turned to the man at my side.

"Thank you.", I told him, "That was awkward."

He laughed. "That is just Albert. He is harmless.", he replied, "You looked like you were going to either faint or bolt out the door, so I figured I better come save you."

I couldn't help but notice his arm was still around me. "I was debating between the two.", I admitted, "Thank you, again. I'm Ray.", I said, extending my hand, which seemed odd considering his arm was draped behind me. He moved his arm, so it would be easier to shake my hand. "I am Jake."

"Not to sound too cliché, but are you new in town? I have not seen you around here before.", he said.

"Not new in town, but very new to a gay bar.", I replied.

"Oh man, is this a gay bar?", he joked, looking around.

"Well, since no one has asked me if they could fuck me a little at Circle K, I have a feeling it is.", I laughed.

"Seriously? I get asked that at Circle K at least three times a week.", he said, smiling.

"I bet you do.", I replied, freezing the moment the words left my mouth. My change of demeanor did not escape Jake.

"Man, this really is your first time in a gay bar, isn't it?", he asked.

"Not my first time, but the last time I was in one, I was with my wife.", I replied.

Jake raised his eyebrows and looked down at my finger; I had not yet taken off my ring.

"Your wife is not with you this time?", he asked, glancing around.

"No. My wife died.", I blurted. That was the first time I had said dead instead of passed. I was not expecting to speak about Sara to anyone here; I wasn't expecting to speak to anyone here at all.

FATE IS NEVER LATE

"I am sorry.", he said; a very sincere look on his face. "Do you mind if I ask what happened?"

I did not want to talk about it, but I could not just brush him off after he saved me from Albert. "She was in a car accident.", I told him.

"I'm sorry for asking.", he said, "There is nothing that could have happened that would not have been tragic. How long ago?",

"A couple years."

"And your still wear your ring?"

"Yes. I cannot bring myself to take it off. If I do, it is like she is really gone.", I admitted.

"I didn't mean to pry.", he said, sincerely.

"It is okay. Everyone I know knew Sara and knows what happened. I have never had to tell anyone what happened."

"Okay, one last question and we will move on to happier topics. Why are you at a gay bar? Are you gay or are you just avoiding women at the regular bars?"

I had to laugh; that was such a legitimate question, but such a loaded one. "I don't know what I'm doing here at all.", I replied, "I just dropped my youngest off at college and did not want to go back to an empty house."

I couldn't decipher the look on his face. "What?", I asked.

"Not many people surprise me.", he said, "You do."

"Is that a bad thing?"

"No.", he laughed, "You are not like most people I meet. I am glad we met."

"Me too. Had we not, Albert would still be trying to fuck me a little.", I replied.

He laughed, placing his hand over mine when he did. I must have paled when he did so, because he quickly retracted it. "I'm sorry. I am just a touchy-feely person. I didn't mean anything by it. I take it you are not gay?", he asked.

I felt bad; I didn't mean to react that way, but it was just instinct. "There is nothing to be sorry for.", I told him, "I am gay...or I was before I was married...I don't know. It's a long story.", I told him.

"Well, you don't want to go home and I would love to hear the story.", he said, calling the bartender over to order us another drink. For the next hour or so, I laid my whole life story out to this total stranger.

Jake hung on every word I said. Having three kids, I was not used to someone actually listening when I talked. When I finished my story, he leaned over and hugged me.

"I am speechless.", he said, "Again, something I am not used to. You are truly unique, Ray."

I laughed. "That may be the first time anyone has called me that.", I said.

 "Well then, maybe this is a night for firsts.", he replied and then he leaned in and kissed me.

My whole body stiffened at first. There were a million things running through my head, but the long ago forgotten sensation of being kissed was fighting them off.

"Was that too much?", he asked, looking in my eyes to gage my true reaction. "No...maybe...I don't know.", I stammered. I had no idea what I truly thought about what just happened.

"I caught you off guard.", he said, You didn't have time to process what was going to happen, but now you do."

He leaned in and kissed me again. This time, I found myself responding to the kiss more than over analyzing it. When we finally pulled apart, I was speechless. However, this time it was because I was still savoring the sensation that I thought I would never experience again.

"I don't want you to do anything you are not ready for," he said, "but you don't want to be alone tonight and neither do I."

My mind was screaming 'no', the butterflies in my stomach were threatening to escape through my mouth; yet, instead, I found myself saying, "We can go to my place."

Jake threw a twenty-dollar bill on the bar and took my hand. "Your car or mine?", he asked.

"You can follow me if you like.", I said, knowing if he got into my car with me, I could never back out of this.

"Sure.", he said, a little disappointed.

The entire way to my house, I was debating trying to lose him. What the hell was I thinking? However, that damn kiss kept replaying in mind. "Maybe we can just kiss some more.", I thought. I thought wrong.

CHAPTER FIVE

When I woke up next to Jake the next morning, I was mentally freaking out. What do I do now? Do I make him breakfast? What is he expecting? Thankfully, I did not have to wonder for long. When Jake woke up, he told me he had to leave. He was helping his sister move and needed to get home to let his dogs out before doing so. He gave me a quick kiss, told me, again, how much he enjoyed meeting me and said he would be in touch.

I peeked through the blinds to make sure he was really leaving. When I could no longer see his car, I slumped to the ground by the window. What had I done? What did this mean? I felt nauseous, but a little relieved and excited at the same time. I had brought a man to my house...to Sara's house...and had sex with him.

I didn't even know him. What if he killed me in my sleep? What if he had some disease. Oh my God, it had been so long since I had to worry about safe sex. Did we do anything that was unsafe?

All I wanted to do was go crawl in bed, fall asleep and forget that last night even happened. However, I couldn't go back to the bedroom; that would only throw the events of last night in my face. Instead, I laid down on the couch and tried to sleep.

I woke up to a call from Vincent. "What are you doing?", he asked.

"Trying to sleep away regret. You?", I answered.

"Oh shit! What did you do? Never mind, I don't want to hear this over the phone, meet us at Starbucks in twenty?"

"Give me forty. The sleep did nothing for the regret, maybe a shower will."

FATE IS NEVER LATE

"See you then."

I got up, took a shower, which also did nothing to wash away the regret, and headed out.

Alan ran up to me before I was fully out of my car. "Who did you sleep with?", he asked, with too much excitement. "What makes you think I slept with anyone?", I asked.

He put his hand on his hip, giving me his best 'bitch please' look. "I know you well enough to know that there are only two things you would regret; getting into an argument with one of your kids or hooking up with someone."

Damn, he was good.

"I will tell you once I have some caffeine in my system.", I told him.

"Well then what are you waiting for, Mary, come on."

He grabbed my arm and pulled me into Starbucks. Vincent shook his head but was smiling from ear to ear.

"So, what happened?", Alan asked.

"Can I actually order first?", I shot back. "Here, take mine.", he replied, handing me his drink, "I want to know now."

"Vincent, go order me another drink.", Alan said.

"Oh hell no, if you think I am going to miss this, you are crazy.", Vincent replied.

"Ugh.", Alan grunted, taking out his phone and placing a mobile order.

"Are you really that lazy?", Vincent sighed.

"Yes, but I want to hear this.", Alan replied.

"Okay. Okay.", I gave in. "As you know, I dropped Destiny off at college yesterday.", I began.

"Boring!", Alan cut in.

I just rolled my eyes.

"Anyway, after I dropped her off, I didn't want to go home to an empty house."

"So, you picked up a hitchhiker and fucked his brains out?", Alan cut in again.

"Alan, let the man talk!", Vincent scolded.

"No. It was not a hitchhiker.", I continued, "I met him in a bar."

Now they were both leaning forward in their seats. "What, no smart-ass comment?", I asked.

"Hell no. Keep on.", Alan said.

"That is about the extent of it.", I said, "I went to a bar and ended up leaving with a guy."

Alan reached across and grabbed my shirt. "If you think we are going to let you leave it at that, you are crazy.", he said. The couple at the table next to us looked over. "Too much espresso.", I told them, nodding my head towards Alan. They rolled their eyes and returned to their conversation.

Knowing I was never going to get a moment of peace until I told them everything; I did. When I was done, they both leaned back. Vincent looked genuinely dumbfounded; Alan had a smile from ear to ear.

"So, how was it?", Alan asked.

"It was different."

"Yes, but different good or different bad?"

I had yet to really contemplate that answer. "Good in an unexpected way.", I admitted.

"See, I told you he would go the gay route.", Alan said to Vincent.

"Yes, Alan. You are always right.", Vincent replied sarcastically. He then turned his attention to me. "Are you okay?", he asked, sincerely.

"I will be.", I replied, "I just have to absorb it all."

"What is there to absorb?", Alan asked, "You have gone years without sex. I can hardly go a full day."

I looked at Vincent, who had a slight blush; the people at the table next to us were looking over again.

"A side effect of the espresso.", Vincent told them. They quickly looked away.

"I never had time for sex.", I said, "I have work and the kids and the house." "Had.", Alan interrupted, "You had the kids. They are all out of the house now, which leaves a lot of space you need to fill. You know, like with strangers from a

FATE IS NEVER LATE

bar." He looked like the cat that ate the canary.

"Gee, thanks for that reminder.", I replied.

"Oh, come on. You dedicated every minute of every day to the kids. I get that. I wish my father would have been more like that.", Alan said, "However, the kids are all at school now and that gives you time to fill in both your schedule and your bed."

"Do you ever think of anything but sex?", I asked him.

"No!", Alan and Vincent answered in unison. We all laughed.

"Are you going to see him again?", Alan asked.

I rotated my head to try and get the kinks out. "I seriously doubt it. I don't think I even got his phone number.", I admitted.

FATE IS NEVER LATE

"Damn, boy, you are a player.", Alan said.

"Yep, that is me.", I replied, sarcastically.

"Well fuck him anyway. There are plenty more men out there.", Alan said, before laughing at his own thought and adding, "Wait, I forgot, you already did that last night!" He continued to laugh at his perceived wit.

"Last night was a one-time thing.", I said.

"With him or in general?", Vincent asked.

"Definitely with him. Beyond that, I really don't know.", I said.

Vincent put his hand over mine. "Look. In all seriousness, I know what a big deal this for you, but it does not have to be a bad thing. You deserve a life. You deserve to be happy.", he said.

"Yeah, I am sure I'm going to be real happy when my dick falls off from some Casanova's STD.", I replied.

"First of all, no one has said Casanova in like 2oo years. Secondly, you did not use protection?", he asked.

"I didn't even think about it. It is not like I had this planned.", I replied.

"Oh brother, we are going to have to set you up with a hookup kit. You know....just in case.", he said.

"Aren't you just the sweet one.", I laughed.

"I do what I can.", he smiled.

"Seriously though, condoms can last up to a year, if you buy the goods ones. You need to have some on-hand, in case another desire to avoid going home arises."

I rubbed my eyes, trying to clear the visual of my sex-kit and the lingering thoughts of Jake, "Fine.", I conceded, "But less than ten items. No way in hell I am going through the cashier line at Walmart with a basket of sex related items."

"Walmart?", Alan shrieked. "No, no, Mary. We are taking you to Todd's."

I scooted back my chair and waived my hands in front of me. "No way! I am not going on a shopping spree at an adult store!"

"You are and you are going to love it there!", Alan replied, giddily.

God help me!

CHAPTER SIX

Even with a fully stocked 'protection-pack', which I decided sounded better than 'sex-kit', I was determined not to repeat the mistake I made with Jake. The idea of dating no longer freaked me out, as it had before. However, I knew that a hookup was not what I wanted.

Begrudgingly, I downloaded a couple dating apps on my phone. It is really cute that they call them dating apps; unless dating now consisted of a car ride from a pickup location to a hook up location, these were far from dating apps.

Most of the conversations went like this:
Them: "What's up?"

Me: "Not much, you?"

Them: "My dick. Wanna help me with that?"

Me: *block user.*

Every so often, you would get someone who must have recently jacked-off because they would go back and forth eight or nine times before they asked if I was interested in a hookup. These were not hookup apps like Grindr either; they were ones like Plenty of Fish and OK Cupid.

Just as I was about to delete the app, a message popped up in my inbox. It was from a guy whose profile I had checked out (and was impressed with) but did not message him for fear that he would be just like the others. If I did not message him, I could always envision that he was actually a nice guy.

The message read:

Justin: "Were you really going to delete the app without talking to me first?"

Me: After looking around the room. "Ummmmm...how did you know I was going to delete the app?"

Justin: "Because you show as someone who 'replies selectively' and I notice you spend less time on the app each day."

Me: "Okay, Justin. You are either psychic or very creepy. How would you know that?"

Justin: "There is about to be a knock at your door."

I froze. Did he know where I live? Was he outside my door?

Justin: "Just kidding! I was pretending to be psychic but reread it and it just sounded creepy."

Me: "Oh My God! You scared the shit out of me. I was already gauging if I could fit under my bed."

Justin: "LOL. I'm sorry. That would have been funny to see though."

Me: "I have to ask, you cannot see me, right?"

Justin: "Not since you put up those dark curtains."

Justin: "I'm just kidding! No. The app shows a green light whenever you are on it. Each night, I notice your light goes out quicker and quicker. I couldn't let you go without saying hello."

Me: "What took you so long?"

Justin: "I really liked your profile, but I figured if I did not message you, I could pretend like you are a nice guy and not a tool like most of the men on here."

I had to laugh out loud when I read that.

Me: "Maybe you are psychic because I thought the same exact thing about you."

Justin: "Great minds think alike."

Me: "That they do."

Justin: "So, before you delete the app and forever erase me into history, I would like to talk to you."

FATE IS NEVER LATE

Me: "My finger is nowhere near the button. Talk away."

And talk he did; we did. We talked for almost five hours that night. The conversation was incredible. I felt like I had known Justin forever. Not one time, in those five hours, was there any mention of a hookup (or anything sexual actually). I was surprised by how freely I shared information with him. I was always very particular with who I shared any information with. I was not sure if I had even told Vincent and Alan some of the things I told Justin.

At the end of our conversation, we agreed to meet at another gay bar in the area. No, I know what you are thinking, I said I was not going to repeat the same mistake I made with Jake. It was not like that. We were going to meet at the bar during the day. Justin wanted to go to a restaurant, but

I was hesitant about being seen in public with a guy.

Considering I went out with Vincent and Alan a couple times a week, I know that was crazy, but this was different; this was more of a date. When we went out, there was no mistaking that Vincent and Alan were a couple. I didn't care if people knew I was out with a gay couple, but I still had this fear of people knowing or thinking I was. Even after the experience with Jake, and seeing how open people were on the app, my mindset was still very much stuck in the past.

When I arrived at the bar, I was relieved to see they had an outdoor patio. If we sat out there, I could pretend like we were not at a bar during the day. I arrived early, so I would not have the awkward moment of entering the bar and having to look around for

Justin. I sent him a text letting him know I was out on the patio.

Five minutes later, the door to the patio opened and out walked Justin. My stomach dropped. He was even better looking in person. It was easy to talk to my phone screen; I was not sure if I could be as confident in person. My fears were quickly quenched when he looked over at me and smiled.

I stood up and he walked over and gave me a huge hug. I let out the breath that I was unaware I was holding. You do not know how many times I wanted to text him to ask him if he was a hand-shaker or a hugger. Believe it or not, I am a hugger, but not everyone is.

"It is so nice to meet you in person.", he said. Even though I was already lost in his blue-gray eyes, I managed to say, "It is nice to meet you too." It seemed such a stupid thing to say, but I was happy I was able to say anything at all.

Our in-person interaction flowed just as easily as our online conversation. It was even better because I was able to hear his voice (which was deep but soft and always had a hint of laughter in it) and see the way his smile lit up those beautiful eyes of his.

We sat there and talked for hours. I did not realize how long we had been talking until the sun began to set. It was then that I realized that he and I had not stopped to eat, go to the bathroom or even order a second drink.

I could have sat there all night, but I knew he worked the night shift. "I am in no way rushing you off, but you need to be at work in two hours. I'm sure you want to eat and need to get changed before your shift.", I said.

He looked down at his watch and I could see the sadness wash over him. "I will grab a protein bar when I go home to change. That will give us another thirty minutes together.", he said.

My heart melted. My brain said I should make him go. He had a twelve-hour nursing shift and it wasn't fair for him, or his patients, if he was weak or disoriented from hunger. That is what my brain said. I wasn't listening to my brain at that moment. My heart was saying, "thirty more minutes-make them count!" "That is the sweetest thing you could have said.", I told him. He blushed.

"I don't want this day to end, but at least I have the goodbye hug to look forward to.", I told him.

"You don't have to wait until I leave for that.", he said, standing.

I stood, as well, and took the step forward that separated us. His arms were soft around me, yet his hands gripped my back as if to hold onto the embrace. I had no intentions on letting go right away. I rested my head in the crook of his neck. He smelled so good. Neither of us pulled away.

Our bodies swayed, slightly, as if lost in a dance; the only music the beat of our hearts. I looked up at Justin, as he looked down at me. Our eyes met, followed closely by our lips. Our lips had no more a desire to part than our bodies had. The kiss led to multiple, our lips never more than a breath from each other. I ran my hands up his chest and rested them upon the stubble on his cheeks. I pulled back, but only enough to look into his eyes.

There was as much compassion as desire reflected in his eyes. I wove my hands through the back of hair and pulled him forward. The kisses grew more intense, but never were they rushed. Our bodies fit together perfectly; there was no feeling of where mine ended and Justin's began.

I always knew that Sara and I were made for each other because of the way our bodies perfectly interlocked when we slept. It was two puzzle pieces fitting perfectly together. The two of us merging into one. I am not comparing this moment with Justin to my life with Sara, however, the connection put my soul at ease and my soul had been in a state of chaos since the day Sara passed.

Justin pulled back slightly and rested his forehead against mine. "I think I have to leave.", he said, frowning.

"I know.", I said, taking his face in my hands. I loved the feel of the stubble on his cheeks and the happiness reflected in those beautiful eyes.

FATE IS NEVER LATE

"Thank you very much for today.", I told him, leaning forward and kissing him softly.

"Are you kidding?", he asked, "It was my pleasure. If you really want to thank me, don't let this be the last time we meet."

His eyes locked on mine. "I really hope it is not.", I said, easily.

"Then it won't be. I will text you later.", he replied, planting a quick by soft kiss on my lips and walking away.

A moment later, a text came through: "I could not look back or I would have never left. Thank you for an amazing day. I hope I don't kill any patients while daydreaming of our next one."

He could probably hear my laugh from the parking lot.

As I drove home, my mind was not the jumble of fear, doubt and regret that I had with Jake. In fact, I had a permanent smile on my face, which I didn't fight like I normally would. I was happy and I was at peace with the happiness. When I laid in bed, it hit me that, for the first time in a long time, I did not sit in my car and stare at the darkened windows. I did not pause at the door before unlocking it; having to will myself to walk in.

As I picked up my phone to text Justin goodnight, a text came through from him. "I have not killed anyone yet. I knew this was a perfect day.", it read.

I didn't think I could smile more than I had; I was wrong. "It was a perfect day, for which I thank you and I add an extra thank you on behalf of your patients.", I replied.

He wrote back, "I will be thinking of you all night, so feel free to dream about me."

"The prospect of dreaming about you is the only thing that will get me to sleep tonight.", I replied.

"Good night and sweet dreams. I will be there waiting for you.", he replied.
"Good night and I shall see you soon.", I sent.

He did not lie; he was in my dream and the dream was as great as the day had been.

CHAPTER SEVEN

Justin and I had three more dates before we ended up in bed together (as well as the shower, kitchen and briefly on the staircase). It was incredible. It felt like it was my first time being with a man.

Yes, I had a boyfriend when I was younger, but at that age you can get off on a kiss. You do not know what making love is about; at sixteen, it is just sex. And, yes, there was Jake, but I was so nervous and wracked with guilt that everything with him was a blur. I never thought it would be possible to make love to a man; I was wrong.

The next seven months with Justin were incredible. Between work and his schooling to obtain his RN, we were not able to get together as often as I would have liked, but a day never passed where we did not text good morning and good night; with many texts in-between.

Thanksgiving was coming up and I was seriously thinking of introducing him to the kids. Granted, they would be surprised, as they didn't even know I have been seeing someone, but it felt right with Justin.

A few nights prior to Thanksgiving, Justin and I were going with Vincent and Alan to Vincent's office holiday party. It was there that I was going to invite Justin to Thanksgiving. I was so nervous. It was a long time before I even introduced Vincent and Alan to the kids and they were my best friends. I knew that Destiny would be ecstatic for me, but I still had no clue how the boys would respond.

After having a fantastic meal of prime rib and scallops, we spent hours on the dance floor. Normally, I was not a dancer. However, I made an exception when it came to slow dancing with Justin. Maybe it was just an excuse to hold him close for a while; maybe he just made it easy for me to step out of my comfort zone.

Halfway through George Michael's "Last Christmas", I whispered in Justin's ear that I wanted him to spend Thanksgiving with me and the kids.

He pulled back and the look on his face was not what I was expecting. "Did you hear me?", I asked him, confused. "Yes.", he replied, "We need to talk." I had spent so much time wondering how the kids would react, and if it was the right thing for them, that I never stopped to consider if maybe it would be too soon for Justin.

"Okay.", I said, "We can talk when we get home." Justin stopped dancing. "Actually, let's go talk now.", he said, taking my hand and leading me away from the dancefloor. We walked to a seating area which was tucked away from the commotion of the party. He sat on the small sofa and patted the seat beside him. I sat, angled, so I was facing him.

"These last seven months have been incredible.", he began, "You have made me feel so loved and so wanted. I have not felt that in so long. I can never thank you enough for that." I went to speak, but he stopped me. "There is something I never told you. My roommate Mark, he and I used to date. We dated for three years. In fact, we were engaged at one point."

"You are roommates with your ex-fiancé?", I asked, dumbfounded. I can't believe I did not know this. I had talked to Mark dozens of times when I was in Justin's apartment. You would think that information would have come up at some point. "Yes. A few weeks after we got engaged, Mark cheated on me. He said he just panicked, but I called it off." I drew my hands onto my lap and scooted back slightly. Justin and I talked about everything; why would he not have told me about this?

"So, he cheated on you, you called off the engagement, but you still lived with him?", I asked.

"Neither of us could afford to move out when it happened.", he said, "I moved into the guest room and we coexisted. He works days and I work nights, so it was not that bad; we hardly saw each other. Over time, we were able to rebuild a friendship."

"You two have always appeared to be good friends.", I said, "So, why are you telling me this now?", I asked.

Justin reached out and took my hands in his. "Mark has been reassigned to Pensacola and he wants me to move there with him."

My first thought was, "Oh my God. Mark is moving and he cannot afford to live on his own. He is going to ask for us to move in together." If only that were the case.

"So, you will need a new place to live?", I asked.

Justin released my hands and rubbed his face. "No. I will have a place. We found a place near the hotel he will be working at."

I was surprised I could feel my heart drop because the rest of my body was in shock. "You are moving?", I asked, "You are moving with a guy you used to be engaged to that cheated on you?"

"He has apologized for that a million times.", Justin said.

"Okay, great. He apologized; you mended your friendship, but to move with him to Pensacola? Why?"

Justin reached for my hand, but I pulled it away. "Mark said that seeing you and I together made him realize what he gave up. He wants another chance. He wants us to get back together."

I leapt up. "Are you fucking kidding me, Justin? You are seriously telling me that you are not only moving away with Mark, but the two of you are getting back together?" He had the audacity to look at me with those puppy dog eyes. "Yes.", was all he replied. I began pacing, mostly so not to choke him.

"So why did you come tonight?", I asked.

"We do not leave for five weeks and I wanted to spend as much time with you as I could.", he replied.

What. The. Fuck! I turned to face him. "Let me get this straight. For the last seven months that we have been together, you have been living with your ex-fiancé. The same ex-fiancé that cheated on you before the wedding. Now, this cheating ex-fiancé realizes the error of his ways and wants you back...and you....and you want him back as well? However, you want to kill five more weeks with me because I make you feel so loved and so wanted? This is what you are telling me?"

"Yes.", he replied, "You are an amazing man. I love the time we spend together and I want to spend what little time I have left with you."

I froze. "Mother fucker, you are not dying of Ebola. As far as I know, you do not have flesh eating bacteria. You have five weeks left because you are moving with your cheating ex to Pensacola so you can rekindle your flame, until such time that he chooses to douse it again! Are you fucking kidding me?"

He stood and reached for my hand, but I stepped back. "Baby, don't be like that. The last seven months have been great and we can have five more weeks of that."

Can you believe this guy? I kid you not- this is what he told me. "Oh, lovely.", I replied, "Maybe if the groundhog of disfunction sees his shadow, we can have six more weeks.", I spat.

"Wait a minute. Have you been sleeping with him?", I asked. Justin looked down and to the left. Take my word on this, people, if you ask someone something and they look down and to the left, their pants are about to catch on fire.

"Oh my God. You have!", I yelled.

"Only for the last couple weeks.", he said.

"You mean the last couple weeks that you have you have also been sleeping with me? We have not used protection in months, Justin. I trusted you and you have been sleeping with your cheating ex-fiancé that is probably riddled with every STD known to man. Get the fuck out!", I yelled.

"He told me his is clean.", was his reply. "Yes, and he also told you he loved you and that you were the only one for him..until you caught him in bed with another guy, right? I don't believe you, why in the hell do you think I would believe him?"

He went to reach for me again; this time I walked away. "Can we talk about this later?", he called.

"Sure, send me post card from Pensacola, fucker!"

FATE IS NEVER LATE

As soon as I turned the corner, my anger gave way to heartbreak. I was waiting to see Rod Serling with a cigarette sticking out of his mouth. Instead, I saw Vincent and Alan and I broke down.

"I will fucking kill him!", Alan said, "Where is he? I will rip his dick off, stick it down his throat, pull it back out and mail it to Mark."

"Alan, we will do no such thing.", Vincent said, "He is not worth the postage. There is an incinerator on the maintenance level. We can take him there."

Somehow, these two managed to make me smile. "It's okay, guys, I will be fine. Is it okay if we go?", I asked.

"After I find him.", Alan said.

"No. You can't. Vincent has to work with these people. For all we know, he may be the one tasked with cleaning the blood out of the carpet."

"Good point.", Vincent said.

"I will throw him out the window.", Alan said, "The city can clean up the blood." The thing is, I did not doubt that we would follow through with it.

"It's not worth it.", I lied, "Let's just get out of here." Vincent and Alan helped me up.

"You are staying at our place tonight.", Vincent said, "I don't want you spending the night alone."

A laugh escaped me. "Not wanting to spend a night alone is what got me into this mess to begin with.", I replied, "I am not going to run from the pain this time. After all, darkness is my old friend."

Vincent hugged me. "Well, call darkness and tell him that he will have to wait because you are crashing at our house tonight.

FATE IS NEVER LATE

CHAPTER EIGHT

I wish I could say that I did not respond like a love-sick teenager. I wish I could say that I did not spend 48 hours in bed, crying. I wish I could say I fought off the darkness. Wish in one hand and shit in the other and see which one gets full first. The day before Thanksgiving, I pulled myself out of bed and spent the next twenty four hours cleaning and cooking. The kids would be here in the morning and there was no way I was going to take away from their Thanksgiving.

I felt even worse because they automatically assumed my haggard appearance and overall sense of morose had to do with another holiday without Sara. I wasn't about to tell them that part of my heart had died and the little piece that remained had just been stepped on.

FATE IS NEVER LATE

To think I was about to introduce that prick to my babies! After dinner, we all went into the kitchen to make figgy pudding. None of us would ever dare eat it, but it was a tradition Sara started after she lost a bet with me that figgy pudding was just an imaginary item in a song.

I went to bed that night numb. However, waking up to the kids being home was the greatest gift I could have. They were on break, so I would have them home for a week. I prepared them breakfast, which they warmed up at around 1pm, when they finally woke up and dragged themselves downstairs.

We were all on the couch watching *Airplane* when my text tone went off. I looked at my phone and saw there was a message from Justin. I went to clear the message, but opened it instead.

"I hope you had a great Thanksgiving. Thinking of you.", it read. I was going to hit delete. Instead, I replied, "I hope you rot in hell or in Pensacola. Either place works for me." I then hit send, went into his contact and clicked on the block option.

"Who was that?", Destiny asked, a sly grin on her face.

"It was Alan.", I lied, proud of my quick thinking.

"Hmmmmm. Seemed pretty intense. He didn't kill anyone did he?", she asked.

I couldn't help but laugh. "Not yet."

"And why did you turn off your phone?"

That girl was too smart for her own good. "Because I didn't want to be disturbed while I am spending time with the loves of my life.", I told her.

"Speaking of.", she said.

"Girl, don't even play me. Watch the movie."

FATE IS NEVER LATE

She smiled and turned back to the tv.

For the remainder of the week, I only thought of Justin when I laid in bed for the night. I found myself talking to Sara about him, which made me smile. With the kids being home, I felt like Sara was there with me as well.

"You know you were the only woman for me.", I told her, "And you will always be the love of my life. Please do not think that I have forgotten you. You are with me every second of every day."

The remote fell off the nightstand, which made me laugh. Sara would always keep the remote on her side of the bed. Every time I asked her for it, she would fumble and the remote would tumble to the ground. I would then have to get up and retrieve it, which would have always been easier to just do from the get-go.

"Some things never change.", I laughed, and I got out of bed to pick the remote up off the floor. I turned off the tv and fell asleep with the remote clutched to my chest.

The day the kids were set to go back to college, Destiny came into my room. "So, anything you want to tell me?", she asked.

"That I love you.", I replied.

She smiled, came up and kissed me and sat next to me on the bed. "I love you too. Anything else though?"

"I love your brothers too.", I said.

She smacked me. "Anything about, I don't know, maybe Justin?"

I froze. "What about Justin?", I asked, wondering how she could possibly know about him. Did he leave something here that had his name on it?

"Dad. I am the one who set up the dating app for you, remember?", she asked, "I may have checked up on you to make sure you were using it."

I felt the color leave my face. "Destiny, please tell me you did not read any of my messages on there!", I exclaimed. "Gross! Of course not!", she replied, "I just signed on one time to make sure you were using it. I was happy to see you had a few messages. The last was from someone named Justin."

I made a mental note to change my password. Actually, I made a mental note to delete the app completely. "I did talk to a couple people; Justin being the last. He turned out to be as big as a whack-job as the rest of them, so that was the last time I used it." Hey, technically that was the truth.

"Dad, I was really hoping you would put yourself out there more.", she said.

If only she knew. "You don't know my life, woman. I have been going out with Vincent and Alan on a regular basis. I am choosing real life over virtual life.", I told her.

"It's the squeaky wheel that gets the grease, dad, not the third wheel.", she said.

"I am getting plenty of grease.", I said, immediately blushing when I realized how that sounded.

"You go, boy!", she said.

"No. No. That came out wrong.", I tried to elaborate.

"Don't worry, dad. You secret is safe with me. I am happy for you." She kissed me on the cheek and left the room.

When the kids left, they took my happiness with them. I thought maybe I was over the craziness of being devastated over a seven-month fling, but that was not the case. The kids were gone, Sara was gone, Justin was gone and, once again, I was alone.

A couple hours after I curled up in bed, my house phone rang. I had forgotten I even had a house phone. I was going to ignore it, figuring it must be a telemarketer. Then I heard Alan's voice on the answering machine.

"I know the kids went back to school today, so get your ass out of bed and into the shower. We are going out tonight.", I heard him say. How the hell did he get my house number? Why didn't he just call me on the cell? Hell, why was he calling me. I don't do phone calls. Why didn't he just text me? That is when I remembered that my phone was powered off. I powered up my phone to see twelve text messages and three missed calls. Thankfully, all from Alan and Vincent.

I texted him back, "How did you get my home number?".

"I had to call my phone from your house that time I couldn't find it. The real question is why the hell have you not responded to my texts or calls?"

I knew if I did not respond, the texts and calls would continue. "My battery died.", I lied.

"Bitch, your battery dying would mean you used your phone a lot and we both know that did not happen. You turned it off to avoid Justin, didn't you? Why the hell have you not blocked him?", he asked.

"Actually, I did block him.", I replied, proudly.

"Good for you. So how long until you are ready?', he asked.

FATE IS NEVER LATE

"By ready, I am assuming you are refereeing to how long until I am ready to fall asleep. The answer to that is about two minutes; assuming texts and calls do not keep me awake.", I replied.

"Look, Mary, we are going out tonight and by we, I mean you and us. Get up, slap on some deodorant and head to our house. We are going to Ybor."

The last thing I wanted to do was to go out, much less to Ybor. "I know the last thing you want to do is to go out, especially to Ybor.", he texted, "Too bad!"

Damn, that man knew me all too well. "Okay, but I actually have to shower, so I will just meet you all there.", I replied. I did have to shower, but I wanted to take my own car, so I could leave when I wanted to. Yes, I knew I would end up staying there until they left, but I could try to fool myself.

I had to admit, it felt good to get out. I decided to switch it up a little and had a glass of wine instead of my usual Corona Light. Big mistake. I had never drunk wine before and had no idea of how it would affect me.

We were hanging out on the patio at *Bradley's*, watching the freak show that is Ybor on any given night, and enjoying each other's company. "Hey whores!", our friend DJ said, coming up to our table. "Where is Justin?", he asked. I broke down crying.

"You prick!", Alan said.

"What? What did I say?", DJ asked.

"He is not with Justin anymore.", he replied.

"Oh no, honey, I am so sorry.", DJ said, hugging me.

"It's okay.", I lied, wiping my eyes.

"You know what you need? You need a shot or five or fireball.", DJ said.

I shook my head because I didn't trust that I could speak without starting to cry again. "That is the last thing I need.", I finally said, "Honestly, I think I just need to go home."

"You are not driving.", Vincent said, "You never drink more than your two complimentary Coronas. I think the wine was stronger than you thought it would be."

Yeah, no shit. "I will call an Uber.", I said.

"Girl, you are not going to take an Uber.", DJ said, "I am about to blow this hostel anyway. I can drive you home.", he offered.

"We can drive him.", Vincent said. "Bitch, please. You know the drag show starts in ten minutes and your wifey here never misses a drag show.", DJ replied.

"I do like the drag show.", Alan said. "Then it is settled. Get your stuff, Mary, we are leaving.", DJ told me.

I hugged Vincent and Alan goodbye, both of which offered again to drive me home, and DJ and I left. "I'm not going to ask you what happened," DJ said on the ride home, "but if you want to talk about it, you know I am here."

I leaned my head against the window and closed my eyes. I knew my silence would not offend him. "I was actually going to text you the other day.", he continued, "I saw a Missed Connection on Craigslist the other day that made me think of you."

"A Missed Connection on Craigslist?", I asked, "Isn't Craigslist where you go to buy a car that will last you a week or to look for a slave that will clean your pool and your feet in the same day?"

DJ slapped my arm. "You are so silly. Although you can find both things on there, there is also a section for people who see each other out in the great big world, but didn't have a chance to talk. It's really cool."

"And you were on there why?", I asked. "Honey, you know how many poor men probably see me on the daily and don't have the opportunity to approach me? I check every so often to see if there is anyone who longs to connect with what they missed out on."

I rolled my eyes. "And what about that made you think of me?", I asked.

"There was one whose title said, 'Jake seeing Daddy'."

My eye roll turned into a glare.

"Are you fucking with me?", I asked.

He held his hands up. "No. No. No. I'm serious. That is what it said.", he said.

"Can you please put your hands back on the wheel?", I begged.

"Girl, I can put on concealer and pluck my eyebrows while driving. Wanna see?".

"No, I want to live if you don't mind.", I said.

"Party popper.", he replied, "Anyway, the ad went on to say that this Jake wanted to reconnect with the daddy he met in the bar. Sound familiar?"

"First of all, I am sure there are many Jakes. Secondly, that term grosses me out to no end. Who the hell has such severe issues that they are going to refer to an older man as their daddy? That is disgusting."

"Don't hate the players, hate the game.", DJ replied, "So, are you going to message him?"

"Are you kidding me? Even if I had any desire to see him again, which I

FATE IS NEVER LATE

definitely do not, him using the term daddy would have shattered that.", I said, the bile rising in my throat.

"Well, if you change your mind, just go to Craigslist and then to Missed Connections. Even if you are just bored, it is fun to read the ads on there."

We could not have gotten home quick enough. I thanked DJ, bolted the door and made a beeline for the bed. "I can't believe I cried in public.", I said to myself. "And daddy? Gross! I am lucky that guy did not kill me in my sleep."

I didn't even turn on the tv; I rolled over and waited for sleep. As usual, instead of sleep, every memory from kindergarten on accosted me. I thought about the time I threw up on Margie's shoes at the skating rink during the first-grade field trip. I thought about the time that my drink shot out of my nose at Cracker Barrel. Apparently, my memories wanted to kick me while I was down.

CHAPTER NINE

I rolled over, picked up my phone and typed in *Craigslist* on Google. I don't know who this Craig guy is, but he wasn't playing. This site encompassed almost every major city in every state.

After about ten clicks, I found *Florida*, then *Tampa*, then *Personals* and finally *Missed Connections*. DJ was not kidding, the subject lines pulled you in. There was everything from, "I hate that I love you" to "Missing the fatty from the bus". Of course, I read both of them. I said a little prayer for humanity after doing so.

I was scrolling down, looking for the post from Jake, when one stood out. It read, "WHY AM I ALL ALONE?". I clicked on it. The post broke my heart. It read, "Why am I all alone? My wife died from cancer three years ago. I was diagnosed, myself, a couple months after. Now I have no one and I am dying alone."

I wanted to reach out and hug this guy. I wished the ad contained a phone number, so I could text him and make sure he was okay. I knew how it felt to lose a wife. I knew how it felt to feel alone. I could not even image battling a terminal disease at the same time. That is when I saw the 'reply' option on the bottom of the ad. I clicked it and it brought up my email with the reply address and subject line already filled out.

I began to send him a message, when I realized that his email address was somehow encoded or assigned by Craigslist, but my email address was showing in the 'From' line. I copied the 'To' line, closed out the email and signed in under my Forfriendship33 account. After all, I had no idea who this person was.

I typed "Alone" in the subject line and composed a short email to him; basically asking him if he was okay. Stupid question, I know, but I was not even sure if this would go through.

A minute later, my email tone sounded. It was a reply. It said, "I am fine. Thank you." I was the master of "I am fine", so I messaged back. "I know you don't know me and I don't know you, but if you ever need to talk, I am an email away. I do not care what time. I know, to some extent, what you are going though."

When five minutes had passed with no reply, I figured I was not going to get one. I was happy when I heard the tone go off. "I am sorry to hear that you can relate to what I am going through. Do you want to talk about it?" I laughed. Here I was trying to help this man and he was seeing if I needed to talk. I wanted to make sure he was okay, so I replied.

To: 48a813ac33510zch4u@reply.craigslist.org

"I do not know what it like to live with a life-threatening disease, but I know what it is like to lose a wife. I lost mine a couple years ago to a car accident. I would not wish that on my worst enemy."

To: Forfriendship33@gmail.com

"I am sorry for your loss. At least I had time to come to terms with losing Abigail. I thought her battle with cancer would kill us both. Sadly, it only killed her. I prayed for death every second since she passed. In a way, I got my wish; I was diagnosed with cancer shortly after. I was hoping for a quicker death, but beggars can't be choosers. It is not the disease that bothers me, it is the fact that I have no one by my side as I die."

To: 48a813ac33510zch4u@reply.craigslist.org

"I am sorry for your loss, as well as your diagnosis. Do you have any family in the area?"

To: Forfriendship33@gmail.com

"My parents are long gone. I have no siblings and Abigail and I never had children. For most of my life, it was just Abigail and me. She was all I ever needed. I never felt alone until she was gone. What about you? Any family?"

To: 48a813ac33510zch4u@reply.craigslist.org

"I do have three children; however, they are grown and off at college. I know what you mean; Sara was my life. I never needed anyone besides her and the kids. Now she is gone and they are away and I am in this tomb I used to call a home."

To: Forfriendship33@gmail.com

"It makes me happy to know that you have children. I bet you are a great father and I'm sure you miss them dearly. I could never miss what I did not have. As for your home feeling like a tomb, image if you knew it actually was one. My only hope, at this point, is that I get to die here. It is not much, but it is so much better than a hospital, hooked up to machines. Although, I do pity the neighbors that will only know I'm gone when the smell drifts to their homes."

To: 48a813ac33510zch4u@reply.craigslist.org

"Oh my God. That was so insensitive for me to refer to my home as a tomb. It's just, when I'm alone in the dark, I can feel the walls closing in on me. I saw this episode of Twilight Zone once where the main character was buried alive. That is how I feel most times. I am Ray, by the way."

To: <u>Forfriendship33@gmail.com</u>

"Nice to talk to you, Ray. I am Gabe. As for the tomb comment, there is no need to feel bad. Is there really much difference between a literal tomb and a figurative one? In our minds, both feel just as real. How long were you married?"

To: <u>48a813ac33510zch4u@reply.craigslist.org</u>

"I was married for twenty years. How about you?"

To: <u>Forfriendship33@gmail.com</u>

"Forty incredible years. Abigail and I grew up next to each other. I knew I was going to marry her when I was five. It took a little longer to convince her."

To: <u>48a813ac33510zch4u@reply.craigslist.org</u>

"Forty years? That is amazing! That is unheard of in this day and age. I wish you two could have had eighty. Did the two of you grow up in Florida?"

To: Forfriendship33@gmail.com

"Forty was just our time together on earth. We will pick up where we left off shortly. Yes, we are native Floridians. Born and raised in Tampa. How about you?"

To: 48a813ac33510zch4u@reply.craigslist.org

"I love your outlook. I take it you believe in God? I was also born and raised in Tampa. We have probably passed each other on the street before. Sara was born in Tennessee, but her family relocated here when she was eight. I always gave her a hard time about it, but truth be told, I love Tennessee. It is the only place, besides Florida, that I could ever call home."

To: Forfriendship33@gmail.com

"I very much believe in God. You would not think so, with what I have been through, but He and I have always been close. If we did pass each other, it would have been a long time ago. I rarely leave the house anymore. We used to love going to Columbia and LaTeresita. Abigail loved Spanish food. Tennessee is a beautiful state. We visited there many times ourselves. What area was she from?"

The 'was' part of his question momentarily knocked the breath out of me. Talking about Sara made it feel like she was just downstairs. I had not spoken to anyone about her in as much detail as I was with Gabe.

To: 48a813ac33510zch4u@reply.craigslist.org

"God and I are the same way. Surprisingly, He did not strike me down after Sara passed. I said a few things to

Him that were not very kind. It is very likely we were in the same place at the same time. LaTeresita was always one of our favorite places. The Minuta there is incredible. Sara always ordered the Ropa Vieja, but there is something about the look of it that weirds me out. Did you all ever try Acho Iris? Very similar place, but it is a mix of Spanish and Chinese. The fried rice is to die for. Sara was from Sevierville, which is not too far from Pigeon Forge."

To: Forfriendship33@gmail.com

"To die for, huh? Maybe I need to try it. Will probably be a better way to go than a morphine overdose. The Minuta is one of my favorites as well. I always order that or the Arroz Con Pollo. I am very familiar with Sevierville. We stayed in a cabin near Dollywood a couple times. Have you ever been there? As for God, trust me, He understands."

To: 48a813ac33510zch4u@reply.craigslist.org

"Gabe, do not think I am going to let that morphine overdose remark pass by. I know how dark things can get and I also know that there are times you think it cannot possibly get darker, yet it does. God gave us Free Will, but He also has a plan for us. Do you really want to stand in the way of His plan? He may understand, but that does not mean He can't get pissed. As for Dollywood...ummmmm..yes! I always told Sara that she was the only woman in my life, but she knew I meant besides Dolly...and Tootie from Facts of Life. They were in my life before Sara."

To: Forfriendship33@gmail.com

"I know who Kim Fields is. I was always more of a Ms. Garret fan though. I believe that is more of an age difference thing though. If I was twenty years younger, Kim Fields would have been a very enticing possibility. I don't know what Sara looked like, but you seem to have good taste in women. How old are you? I am sixty-three. As for my morphine comment, If I were going to end my life, I would have done it the moment Abigail passed. I will admit, it is nice to know I have the option."

To: 48a813ac33510zch4u@reply.craigslist.org

"I could never get pass Ms. Garret's voice. Could you imagine that next to you in bed every night? Sara's beauty put Dolly and Tootie to shame, but please never tell either of them that. Since you mentioned my taste in women, there is one thing I may as well tell you. Hopefully it will not matter, but I completely understand if it does; I have dated women and men. I am forty-three. As for your options, please know that contacting me is a very viable option now as well."

To: Forfriendship33@gmail.com

"Abigail sounded a little like Ms. Garret; don't ever tell her I told you that either. As for who you are attracted to, could you imagine if we were all attracted to the same thing? You would have five percent of the population that people found attractive and ninety-five either very lonely or settling. Your being attracted to men and women should be no more unsettling than if you told someone you found both blondes and brunettes attractive. I have never understood why anyone would care about someone's sexuality. As my neighbor's kids say, "You do you boo." Forty-three? I remember those days well. I know it may not seem like it now, but there is a lot of life ahead of you. Our age difference alone is half of your life. Think about all you have done and experienced in half of your life. If I did not have this cancer eating away at me, I would have, at least, twenty more years ahead of me as well. As for the option, thank you, I will use it."

FATE IS NEVER LATE

To: 48a813ac33510zch4u@reply.craigslist.org

"Wow. That is a good way to look at it. It's weird though. I don't know if that shows how much time we, potentially, have or illustrates how quickly time flies. Maybe both? I could not agree more regarding sexuality. The only complication is not knowing if the other person is gay as well. However, even with that, if someone approached me, man or woman, and I was not interested, I would be flattered. All it takes is a simple 'I am not gay, interested, etc.' and move on with your life. I find it laughable that men, especially, think that every gay man is automatically attracted to them. Honey, you don't have women that are attracted to you, what makes you think that is any different with men? If they only knew that gay men hardly like each other."

To: <u>Forfriendship33@gmail.com</u>

"Ray, I really appreciate you reaching out to me; you are the only person who replied to my post. Honestly, I didn't really expect anyone to. It was just my way or getting my feelings out into the Universe. I am glad the Universe delivered my message to you. I must get some sleep now, but I do hope we speak again soon."

To: <u>48a813ac33510zch4u@reply.craigslist.org</u>

"Sara and I always believed that everything happens for a reason. As I am sure you can image, I have doubted the validity of that, many times, over the years. Maybe there is still some truth to it? Get some sleep and we will talk more tomorrow if you are up to it. Good night and sweet dreams."

CHAPTER TEN

When I woke up the next morning, the first words out of my mouth were not, "Oh Shit". I was not thinking about how I was going to get out of bed and muster the energy to make a pot of coffee, which I knew was the only thing that would get me out of bed in the first place. I was not thinking about how many hours I would spend, with said pot of coffee, hoping I would build the energy required to take a shower and contemplate anything taking place outside my front door. Instead, I woke up with a smile recalling my conversation with Gabe.

I felt like I had an amazing conversation with someone I had known all my life. When I thought about the fact that I had no idea who Gabe was, I laughed out loud. I was able to connect with a total stranger on a level that I was not even able to connect with my closest friends.

Perhaps it was because we both shared one of the greatest pains someone can experience. Perhaps it is because we were both at such a low point that we were beyond caring what the other person thought. However, I did not think either was true. I, truly, felt like we were destined to meet.

We discussed things that we couldn't discuss with other people. Not that we couldn't, but that we didn't; either because we knew they really did not want to hear about it, they never asked about it or because we really didn't want to talk with them about it.

See, the burden of loneliness is not always something we choose; it is normally something that just happens. However, is it never a one-way street.

Gabe reached the point where he felt he needed to call out to someone-anyone who could let him know that his voice could still be heard. Not from the voice that spoke from him mouth, but from his soul. Until speaking to him, I did not acknowledge how much I needed that as well.

I wanted to reach out to Gabe; ask him to meet for lunch or coffee. I wanted to continue our conversation in an old-school manner; physical- not just virtual.

I was surprised by this desire, as the thought of even speaking to someone on the phone is normally too much for me to bear. I hated the coldness of texting when it was first introduced. However, without texting, I would probably never speak to anyone.

Does that mere fact contribute to my sense of loneliness? I am sure it does. Yet, I can justify it to myself with the thought that anything is better than nothing.

I booted up my laptop, opened my email and reached out to Gabe.

To: 48a813ac33510zch4u@reply.craigslist.org

"Good Morning. I was wondering if you would like to meet, in person, today. It would be nice to continue our conversation."

To: Forfriendship33@gmail.com

"Morning, Ray. You are trying to hit on me, aren't you? Just Kidding! Today is not a good day. Woke up feeling a little under the weather. A rain check?"

133 | P a g e

To:48a813ac33510zch4u@reply.craigslist.org

"I am sorry you are not feeling well. I will hold you to that rain check. At least, even when you are not feeling well, you keep your wits about you. I normally need a pot of coffee and two cigars before I can function near that level."

To: Forfriendship33@gmail.com

"Two cigars? I am sure I am not the first to tell you this, but you should really give up that habit. My Abigail smoked for about ten years. She quit a long time before she was diagnosed, but it was still lung cancer that took her from me."

To:48a813ac33510zch4u@reply.craigslist.org

"Believe me, I wish I could quit. It is a disgusting habit, which I fully recognize. However, to be honest, smoking is the only thing that allows me to function. Well, that and coffee. I did not begin smoking until Sara passed. Maybe,

FATE IS NEVER LATE

subconsciously, I was trying to be destructive. That could be the case. All I know is that every puff of the cigar bought me a couple extra minutes of life and sanity; even through my mind knew it was taking both from me in the long term. It is now more of a habit, but one that I still desperately need to get by. There are many ways things that people use to cope and survive; cigars seemed like the least evil or the vices."

To: Forfriendship33@gmail.com

"I am not your momma, so I will not lecture you about it, but that does not mean I will not continually suggest that you quit. Not to be harsh, but do you really want to put your children through what I am going through?"

To:48a813ac33510zch4u@reply.craigslist.org

"Gabe, I know this may not make much sense, but, since Sara died, my life has been lived from minute to minute. If smoking is what it takes to give me an extra minute, then that is what I have to do. I have to worry about being here for my kids, right now. As we both know, all too well, tomorrow is never promised."

To: Forfriendship33@gmail.com

"Touché. As I said, I won't hound you about it. We each do what we must to survive. Just something to think about. So, tell me about these kids of yours."

To: 48a813ac33510zch4u@reply.craigslist.org

"I believe I mentioned, I have three. Two boys and a girl. These kids are the best things that ever happened to me; they are my life. They are incredible. All three are off at college. Sara and I hoped that they would be close if they were close in age. We got our wish. Don't get me wrong, sometimes they fight like cats and dogs, but they have each other's back without question.

Donovan is my oldest. Devin is the middle child and Destiny is my baby. And, no, we never set out to go with all "D" names; it just worked out that way. Their names seem to fit their personalities well though; or maybe it is the other way around. I have always believed that a person's name somehow shapes their character. Just an example, and not to be mean, but have you have ever met a Eugene that was not somewhat of a nerd? I always thought my name was so plain; Sara did as well. That is why we wanted to make sure our kids had names they would like. Names they could be proud of. At least, I hope they do."

To: Forfriendship33@gmail.com

"I understand. Those are very strong names you chose for your children. They sound like great kids and, since they are all in college, you must have done something right. If that something began with the names you chose, good for you...and them. Remember, a rose by another other name would smell just as sweet. Don't discount your or Sara's many contributions as to how your kids turned out. I am very happy to hear that, despite the loss of their mother, they still went on to college. A loss of a parent could easily derail a child. The strong names you choose do seem fitting for the will they possess."

To:48a813ac33510zch4u@reply.craigslist.org

"I am still stunned they did so. I tried to make life as normal as possible for them, after Sara passed, but I was on autopilot for so long. I focused on making sure they knew how much I loved them while making sure I did not smother them. They were all I had; I wanted to make sure I was not all they had."

To: Forfriendship33@gmail.com

"As you know, I am not a parent, but I had the most amazing Father anyone could ask for. I know he did everything he could for me and it sounds like you did the same for your kids. What college are they going to? What are they majoring in?"

To: 48a813ac33510zch4u@reply.craigslist.org

"I hope I have done right by them. I pray I always will. They are going to Florida State University. Donovan is an Arts major. He has always been so talented and insightful. Devin wants to be a dentist. Keep in mind, I could never get this kid to brush his teeth- much less floss. Destiny is going for Business Management. She is not yet sure what type of business she wants to run, but I have no doubt that whatever she decides will thrive. There is nothing that can stand in that girl's way."

To: Forfriendship33@gmail.com

"Your children seem to know what they want and have very good heads on their shoulders. Perhaps Destiny can manage Devin's dental practice and Donovan can provide the artwork and interior design. It sounds like your kids would enjoy contributing to each other in that way. What do you do for a living? I was a guidance counselor. Not many would consider it a glorious job, but knowing you helped someone find their path is the most rewarding job I could think of."

To: 48a813ac33510zch4u@reply.craigslist.org

"It is funny how well you know my children from just the little I have told you. They have discussed the very scenario you mentioned. I would love for the three of them to be able to work together in some aspect. We have always been a very close family. My greatest fear, when Sara passed, was that would change. It fills my heart seeing they are still so close. I think being a guidance counselor is an amazing job. Everyone needs guidance; so many don't get it. I am a financial analyst. It is not a thrilling job, by any means, but it always paid the bills."

To: Forfriendship33@gmail.com

"Do not worry about your children remaining close. They all went to the same college, after all. They sound like smart kids and I am sure they had a choice between many colleges. Yet, they all chose the same one. That says a lot. As for your job, or my job for that matter, our job is what we do. Who we are inside is what determines our value. You are very valuable; never doubt that."

To: 48a813ac33510zch4u@reply.craigslist.org

"Thank you for saying that. It is very easy to forget sometimes. So, tell me more about you. What do you enjoy doing?"

To: <u>Forfriendship33@gmail.com</u>

"No need to thank me; I call it as I see it. As for what I enjoy doing? I don't know if I even recall. The last ten years have been spent taking care of Abigail and now myself. It is hard to recall what life was like before her diagnosis. Now, I spend a lot of time reading and cooking. I rarely cooked when Abigail was alive; she loved to do it. She used to make the most incredible cornbread. After she passed, I made it a point to learn how to cook it. I felt if I could do that, I could ensure I kept part of her alive."

To:<u>48a813ac33510zch4u@reply.craigslist.org</u>

"What an incredible tribute to her! I hope to get to taste it sometime. I love reading as well. In fact, I recently joined a book club of sorts. Have you ever heard of MeetUp.com? If not, you should look into it. It is a site that has groups for every type of hobby or interest you can imagine. Some a little more out there than others. The book group was my first real outing since Sara passed. It was nice. You should check it out."

To: Forfriendship33@gmail.com

"I am sure the day will come where you can taste it. The only one I have let taste my cornbread, besides my neighbors, as I normally cook far too much for me to eat alone, is Stella. Stella is a waitress at a diner I go to from time to time. The first time I went, she suggested the cornbread; said she made it herself. It was good, but I could not pass on the opportunity to have her taste Abigail's. The next time I went in, I took her some and she loved it. I take her some every time I go now. Sweet lady. Always thanks me with a hug. You do not find many people who can express compassion like that to someone they hardly know."

To:48a813ac33510zch4u@reply.craigslist.org

"Stella sounds like a sweet woman. We need more sweet people in the world. It seems like everyone has lost their minds; especially lately. It is like all these decent, possibly caring, people were going about their daily lives, but deep down they were just waiting for an excuse to release their hate and anger. Have you seen the movie *The Purge*? I don't think we are too far off from something like that becoming a reality. I believe a lot of it has a lot to do with social media. It is insane how something that connected us like never before has, in turn, caused the greatest disconnection. It is not just kids either. Say what you want about millennials, but they seem to hold their composure better than adults when it comes to social media. I love the idea behind Facebook, but for the five percent of benefit it has, it seems to contain ninety-five percent hate and bitterness. And don't even get me started on the format of it all. You have adults posting items with words misspelled and no punctuation. I can only image the number of teachers that cry themselves to sleep after spending five minutes on Facebook. I have never understood the point of Twitter and Instagram; however, maybe I just realized it. On Instagram, people can allow a photo to speak the proverbial 1000 words, which they would butcher if they tried. With Twitter, they only need to post a sentence at a time, if that. They still butcher it, but it is a lot less painful than their attempt at a full paragraph. Sorry for the rant; I could go on for days about social media. Yet, if not for it, I would not even be typing you now."

To: Forfriendship33@gmail.com

"Something tells me you have conflicting feelings about social media. Ha ha. I had to wipe the emotional skid mark off my monitor. I have never been a big fan, or participant, of social media. Facebook allowed me to let many distant relatives and friends know about Abigail's passing. I was against the idea because, the way I look at it, if they were not close enough to us to know about her disease and death, why would they need to know. A gentleman I used to work with convinced me to do it. I do not regret it, but I have also not logged back on since the initial post. If anyone wanted to reach out to me, I am pretty sure they still sell pencils and stationery. Last I checked, Hallmark was also still in business. Of course, that would require someone to put lead to paper and, God forbid, go looking for the all elusive stamp. It saddens me that this generation may never know what it is like to receive a handwritten letter in the mail. Something that you can hold and, after, save in a drawer. A piece of someone's heart and soul put on paper. Technology, like social media, has many benefits and many disadvantages."

To:48a813ac33510zch4u@reply.craigslist.org

"I hate to be the one to break this you, Gabe, but did you know they do not even teach cursive in schools anymore? Cursive! Gone! Do they not realize that makes a signature obsolete? Kids are going to revert to placing an "X" in the signature line. When I took Destiny to get her driver's license, they asked her to sign (on a digital screen, of course). She wrote her name on the line. Wrote. Her. Name.   They lady behind the computer did not even flinch. I told Destiny she needed to sign her name and she told me that is how they sign it in school. Knowing that the people behind me at the DMV would not appreciate a rant on the difference between printing and signing one's name, I asked the employee if this was common. She told me that she has not seen a signature, for anyone under twenty-five, in years. My heart hurts just thinking about that. I love to write. I would be happy to send you a handwritten letter. Could you image, though, if we had to communicate via 'snail mail' exclusively. Our two days of conversation would have taken months. So yes, technology is a double-edged sword. If you do not mind providing me with your address, I will write you a letter tonight."

To: Forfriendship33@gmail.com

"I have seen news programs regarding this 'new math' they are making the kids learn, but I did not know they have eradicated cursive from the curriculum. How is that even possible? How on God's Green Earth did anyone allow that to happen? Could you image if our forefathers had printed the Declaration of Independence? My God, are kids even able to read what is written there? You have, seriously, made my head spin. I cannot even fathom that anyone in the educational system approved this. What are children being taught now? Are children still required to take English in college? If so, do they still have essays to write? Are they allowed to turn in an essay that is in print? I may have to take a nap after learning this. As for that letter, my address is: 3612 E 138th Ave. Tampa, FL 33613."

To: 48a813ac33510zch4u@reply.craigslist.org

"I am sorry to have broken that news to you. Trust me, I know how you feel. As for the essays in school, not to cause you further dismay, but they don't even hand write them anymore. All papers must be typed. Thankfully, and sadly, computers have spell and grammar check. Therefore, teachers are given papers where they can, hopefully, make out what the kids are saying. I will let you go, so you can take your nap. I will use the time to write you a, old school, letter. Is it sad that I am excited to do so? Look forward to talking more soon."

As soon as I sent Gabe the final message, I went to my drawer and found my old stationary under a dozen knickknacks. Sadly, it took me much longer to find an actual pencil. Once I had both in hand, I sat down and wrote Gabe a very long letter. Believe it or not, I even had stamps. Of course, I had to put multiple on the envelope, as the stamps I had were seventeen cents and the price of postage was now forty-six cents. That really made me realize how long it had been since I mailed a letter, or anything for that matter, out. As I placed it in the mailbox, almost forgetting you had to raise the little flag if you had outgoing mail, I couldn't help but think, "Prime would get this to him in two days.". God help us!

CHAPTER ELEVEN

Gabe and I talked every day and it was the highlight of my day. Sometimes we would exchange one or two messages; other days we would spend most of the day messaging each other. About a week after I mailed him the letter, he informed me that it was received and it brought light to the darkness. I loved to hear that. I felt like I was able to share a more intimate part of myself with Gabe by sending the letter.

Vincent and Alan noticed the change in my demeanor. They continually asked me who the new man or woman was in my life, as surely there must be one. I don't know why, but I did not tell them about Gabe. I think part of me did not because I knew what they were thinking did not apply with us. However, truth be told, what I had with Gabe was very special to me. I wanted it to remain something that just between the two of us. I love Vincent and Alan, but Gabe could understand parts of me that they never could.

It wasn't until they asked me about having someone in my life that I realized I had not even thought about Justin in weeks. It's weird because part of me now realized that I deserved so much better than him; the other part was pissed that I still felt hurt thinking about what happened.

I will admit, I searched for him on Facebook. I laughed out loud when I say his relationship status said "single". I have heard that lie before. Part of me took pleasure in thinking that he had moved away only to be dumped by his ex again. I had no intention on verifying if that occurred. Karma can handle that one.

Thinking about Justin led me to thinking about the app we had met on. I had not been on the app since I met Justin. Against my better judgement, I reinstalled it and signed on. For good measure, I changed my password. I know Destiny would not snoop through the app, but better safe than sorry.

I would not be able to talk to anyone on there if I thought she may see it. Not that I would say anything to anyone that could not be seen by her; I have more class than that. I would just feel as though everything I was typing was geared towards her and not the person.

I had multiple messages. A quick glance showed that seventy five percent of them were for people that were two hours or more away. I didn't even recognize the name of some of the cities a few were from. It may be wrong, but I did not bother with those. If I could not make plans to meet someone for dinner, after work, I could not envision anything serious coming of it.

A couple were from people who were way out of my age bracket. From speaking to a couple of the younger guys, I quickly realized the topics of conversation are very limited. I wanted to find someone closer to my own age. Someone who had similar life experiences that I could also grow old with; not that I did not feel 100 years old already.

That left me with three possibilities. After reading their profiles, I did not believe I would have anything in common with two of them. I messaged them back anyway. First, you never know and secondly, it just felt so rude to let the message go with no reply. As it turned out, my instincts were correct; I had nothing in common with the two and the messages quickly ended.

I had also sent a message to the third person. After two days with no reply, I figured they had either lost interest or met someone. Three days after my message, he replied.

His name was Brian. He seemed like a really nice guy. We messaged back and forth for a week before we decided to meet for dinner. We picked a bar that also sold burgers and wings. Neither of us were big drinkers, but we knew the bar would be empty during the week, which would provide a semi-private place to get to know each other better. The date seemed to go very well. We never ran out of things to talk about, which is always my worst fear.

During our conversation, he mentioned a few things that "we really needed to do together". I took that as a good sign that Brian was looking for something long term and, although what happened with Justin had left me gun-shy, the prospect had me a little hopeful.

We ended the evening with a sweet hug and kiss on the cheek. I thought that was cute as well. By time I arrived at home, I had a message from Brian saying he had a very good night. I replied that I did as well and looked forward to seeing him again. That was the last I heard from him.

The next morning, I sent him a 'good morning' text. No reply. I understand that he may not be hoovering over his phone, waiting for a message, so I did not think anything of it. However, two days passed with no reply.

Needless to say, I was totally confused. I kept replaying the date in my mind to think of something I may have missed. I text him two days later to ask if he was okay. Still nothing.

I was, genuinely, worried that something may have happened to him, but I did not want to seem like I was hounding him. I opened the app to see if, perhaps, he had messaged me on there. There was no message, but his light was green, which meant he was online. A minute later, the online indicator turned off. So, he was alive, but for some reason not messaging me.

The fact that he did not message me did not bother me as bad as the fact that I had no idea why. However, I refused to let it bother me further. He was a nice guy, but it was not like we were in a relationship.

The date was nice; if for some reason it was not as nice for him, that was on him- not me. What did come from it, was absolutely no desire to go back on the app. Mentally, I could not go through the whole process of the 'getting to know you better' part of the conversations, which lasted for ten minutes to one day and just died there.

To:48a813ac33510zch4u@reply.craigslist.org

"Hello my friend. So, I went on a date a couple days ago. All seemed to go well and then I never heard from again. I did not miss the dating scene, nor do I understand it now. People have lost their minds in the last couple decades. The ironic thing is that I really was not looking to date. After talking with Vincent and Alan, I decided to give it another try. I am going to have to convince them (and Destiny) that am I perfectly content with being single. Not only is the dating scene insane, but there are also diseases and things to worry about now. I went too long without having to worry about any of that. Ain't nobody got time for that. 😊 Have you dated since Abigail passed?"

To: <u>Forfriendship33@gmail.com</u>

"Before I begin, you will be proud to know that I got the 'Ain't nobody got time for that' reference. As for your date, I am very sorry to hear that it turned out poorly. Better you find out sooner rather than later. It is his loss- remember that! I never considered dating, as I had the love of my life and lost her. However, when I was first given my diagnosis, I panicked and allowed myself to be set up on a blind date. I did not want to put anyone though what I went through with Abigail, but the thought of going through it alone scared the hell out of me. The lady was sweet, but how should I put this...batshit crazy. I did not try again after that. I understand what you are saying regarding being happy being single, however, it is completely different for me. I am older than you are and I also have a terminal illness. It is easy to accept being alone when you know it will not be for long. You have a lot of life ahead of you, God willing. Don't give up quite yet."

To:<u>48a813ac33510zch4u@reply.craigslist.org</u>

"Don't get me started on your age. You act like you are eighty, which is still almost twenty years away. Remember when you told me that twenty years was a very long time? As for the cancer, I never wanted to ask, but are you undergoing chemo or radiation for it? Medical miracles happen all the time. Big Pharmaceuticals cannot keep burying the cure for cancer. Eventually, someone is going to be able to go public with a cure. Have you ever seen that movie about the Greek wedding? Maybe it is as simple as spraying Windex on yourself. Have you tried that? I'm sorry. I think you know me well enough by now to know that I am not trying to make light of the situation. I recently watched a documentary on the benefits of marijuana and it got me thinking of how many other simple items may have similar qualities. I have not smoked pot since I was a kid, but I believe I would if I was diagnosed with a condition-especially one as severe as cancer. Pot will not kill you and you know what they say- what does not kill you makes you stronger."

To: Forfriendship33@gmail.com

"Did you think I did not notice that you completely changed the topic regarding you dating and remaining single? I didn't; just so you know. I will let it slide- for now. As with many types of cancer, I could have tried chemo and radiation; however, I saw what that did to Abigail. What good is more time if that time has no quality of life? As for marijuana, do you really think I could type this much without it. Ha ha. I believe in natural remedies. I know there is a stigma associated with marijuana, but that is because most of it has other chemicals and items mixed with it. That is never good, regardless of if it is mixed with a plant or food. I believe God provides us with all we need. It is man who alters the creation to try and 'improve' it. Marijuana is a plant and nothing more. If I were to smoke a dandelion, which we always had in the house, as it was Abigail's favorite flower, people might look at me like I was crazy, but I would not be arrested for it. Without the additions, marijuana is just another plant. A plant whose stigma caused its healing properties to be overlooked for a very long time. What it boils down to is 'everything in moderation and as needed'. Besides a few studies regarding wine, alcohol has no medical benefit what-so-ever. It takes and destroys lives, yet it is legal. The same with cigarettes and those cigars you love so much. Why are they accepted? Because they are huge money makers and man loves his money. I'm sure as soon as the government finds a way to make money off marijuana, it will be as widely accepted as alcohol and tobacco. We are seeing the beginning of that movement already. Excuse me while I go find the Windex."

To:48a813ac33510zch4u@reply.craigslist.org

"If the Windex works, I say we buy up stock in it now and then take the information public. I bet you there were many people who tried it after that seeing that movie. I agree with everything you said and I understand about the quality of life issue. I believe there are natural remedies that can heal without causing further harm. As for the dating, I will not ignore the topic. I am, honestly, very happy being on my own. Not having the kids here is a huge adjustment and I miss them every day, but there is a huge difference between missing them and needing a significant other in my life. I need to discover who I am, without Sara, before I worry about incorporating someone else. There are times when I instinctively turn to tell Sara or the kids something and they are not there and that hurts. But does it hurt enough to try to rush into or force something? No. I would rather be alone than be with the wrong person. Remember when we were kids and finding someone, a friend or even someone we were interested in, was so easy? You saw someone you liked and you just went up and talked to them. It's a shame that adulthood steals that purity from us."

To: <u>Forfriendship33@gmail.com</u>

"A shame it is. It does not necessarily need to be that way though. You can still approach someone and start up a conversation. It may not be as effortless as it was as a child, but improbable is not to be confused with impossible. You know what they say, 'Even a broken clock tells the correct time twice a day.' You have to go for it. You will find your 10:15 eventually."

To:<u>48a813ac33510zch4u@reply.craigslist.org</u>

"Excuse me, Mr. Words of Wisdom, but I am pretty sure it was your ad that I responded to and not vice versa. I believe we may have a case of not practicing what we preach here. Ha ha.

I have not given up; I am just pacing myself. I find myself at around 1:18; there is a long way between there and 10:15."

To: Forfriendship33@gmail.com

"Touché. I know what it feels like to be alone and lonely and I don't want you to feel that. You need more than the ramblings of an old man to occupy your time. You see what I did? I added to our clock analogy. Just in the nick of time too. Okay, I will stop. Talking about the time though, I should get to bed. I do not want the other seniors to know I am still awake. Once you get branded a rebel, it is not an easy label to shake. Good night, my friend. We shall speak more tomorrow."

CHAPTER TWELVE

While having my coffee the next morning, I deleted the dating app from my phone. I had four of five messages each day, but they were either from people that were way too far away to date or from people out of my age range.

I used to feel bad and reply to every message, but, apparently on dating apps, that gives the message you are interested. I found that trying not to hurt people's feelings, by not replying, only hurt them more by replying later having to tell them you are not interested.

It is not that I am picky. I just don't see how I am going to have a relationship with someone who lives four hours away. Sure, it would work on the weekends, assuming neither of us had to work; however, there would never be a chance to just see each other during the week and that would be disappointing.

I would have nothing in common with people twenty years younger than I was and I would not have enough time left with people twenty years older than me. Have I mentioned dating (or trying to) sucks?

The book club was meeting tonight, so I decided I would grab a bite to eat before the meeting and then go to the local coffee shop after the meeting. Three outings in one day. I was proud of myself.

I could not image being the person who was sitting by himself in a restaurant, so I chose a nice little deli that had tables outside. I knew I would be more exposed outside, so I ordered two glasses of water. When people walked by, it looked like I was just waiting for someone. Pitiful, yes, but it worked. Hey, it's better than eating at home before I went.

The book club was great. Everyone really enjoyed reading "Gris Gris". I was happy that my first suggestion went over so well. Many people wanted to read the next book in the series, "Legend of the Loa", but 'it was against the book club rules'. Apparently, variety was the spice of life when it comes to book club. That was okay with me; I had read the entire series multiple times.

After the meeting was over, a couple members decided to go for coffee. Of course, during the course of the night, I was asked about my wife. Since I still wore my ring, it was bound to be brought up. It was hard to talk about it with strangers, but having talked to Gabe about it made it easier.

Everyone was very supportive and understanding. Once they found out it was a couple years ago, that Sara passed, one of the members, Bridget, started to get a little too supportive. I did not want anything to interfere with book club, as I really enjoyed it, so I dropped the gay bomb.

Amazingly, it went over much better than I anticipated. Bridget stated that I had been with a woman before, therefore, there was no reason not to do so again. When I told her that I already had the only woman I would ever love in my life, she backed off.

All the "awwwws" from the other women helped. I wasn't being noble; just honest. It may make no sense at all, but knowing I would not be dating another woman made it feel less like I was cheating on Sara.

When I got home, I pulled up my email, but there was no message from Gabe. I hoped his day was as full as mine, but it was also a little concerning. I never wanted him to feel obligated to message me, so I sent a simple email.

To:48a813ac33510zch4u@reply.craigslist.org

"Hello Gabe. I just wanted to let you know that I spent a good portion of the day out and about and it was very nice. I hope you have had a wonderful day as well."

When I awoke the next morning, I checked my email right away. No reply from Gabe. I said a quick prayer for him and went about my day. Later that afternoon there was still no email. The same when I went to bed for the night.

FATE IS NEVER LATE

Of course, Gabe and I had gone a day without talking before, but it was usually known that would be the case. I would be lying if I said I was not worried.

The next morning; nothing. I thought about driving by his house, as I had his address from the letter I mailed him, but that just seemed to be crossing a line. Even if I only looked for a car (which I didn't even know if he owned one) or some activity in the window; it was all too stalkerish. I sent him another quick email just letting him know that I was thinking about him and hoped all was well.

After two more days without hearing from him, I was extremely worried. I thought about calling the hospitals, but what would I say? "Ummmm..excuse me, but do you have a patient there named Gabe?"

I decided I would drive by his house. I would not stop unless something seemed out of place. I don't know what I expected to see that was out of place, but I would have to just trust my gut.

As I was scrolling through the emails, looking for the address, the tone which alerts me of the arrival of an email went off. It was Gabe.

To: Forfriendship33@gmail.com

"Hello my friend. I am sorry if I have had you worried. I was in the hospital for a couple days. It is nothing to worry about. I woke up with a fever that was a little too high for my liking. When I got up to fetch a cold washcloth, I took a little bit of a tumble. Again, nothing major happened but I thought it best to get checked out. I hope I did not worry you too much."

To:48a813ac33510zch4u@reply.craigslist.org

"Oh my God, Gabe. Are you okay now? Are you back at home? I am not going to lie; I was very worried. In fact, and allow me to apologize in advance, I was just heading out to drive by your house to see if anything seemed out of place. I hope you know that I would never disrespect your privacy like that, but I had a feeling something was wrong."

To: Forfriendship33@gmail.com

"You are too kind. I am afraid you would have wasted the trip. I am not in the hospital, but I am also not at home. A former coworker of mine lives near the hospital and was going to be out of town for a couple days. He offered his home to me, so I would be close to the hospital in the even that anything occurred again. In return, I am watering his plants and, hopefully, keeping his fish alive. Honestly, I am fine. It was nothing major; they just wanted to monitor me for a couple days. I feel much better now."

To:48a813ac33510zch4u@reply.craigslist.org

"Please know you can always contact me if you need anything. It does not matter what time of the day or night. I am not asking for yours in return, but I am going to give my cell phone number in case you ever need it. It is 813-505-XXXX. Do not hesitate to use it. I don't believe I ever asked you, but do you have a car? Are you able to get any supplies you need for the time you are at his house? Do you need anything from your house?"

To: Forfriendship33@gmail.com

"If I didn't know you were a father before, I would definitely know now. Haha. I do not own a car, but I really have no use for one. I never stray too far and the ambulance driver was very accommodating 😊. My coworker,

Michael, picked up some clothes and my laptop for me. If I need food, there are ample delivery places nearby and I hear that some grocery stores now deliver right to your home. I thought the idea was preposterous when I first hear it, but maybe they may be on to something."

To: 48a813ac33510zch4u@reply.craigslist.org

"Gabe, please allow me to provide you with your dinner tonight. If you wish to have groceries delivered today, that is good, but it is already late in the evening and I want to ensure you have a good meal for tonight. All I need is the address; I promise I will not show up unannounced. I have a gift card to DinnerDash that is about to expire and there is no way I can use it all on just myself. I will have something delivered to me, as well as to you, and then the card will not go to waste."

I did not have a gift card, but a little white lie wouldn't hurt.

To: Forfriendship33@gmail.com

"I know that if I say no, you will not let it go so easily, so, instead, I will say thank you. It has been a trying day and not having to worry about what I am going to eat will be very helpful. I could barely stomach the food they served in the hospital. The address is 33 Sanchez St. Tampa FL 33605. Anything you send you will be fine; I am not a picky eater. This food will be appreciated more than you may know. Thank you very much."

To: 48a813ac33510zch4u@reply.craigslist.org

"Your acceptance is thanks enough. I am happy to be able to help in some way. And this is not totally selfless, as I am hoping for some cornbread in return some day. I just placed the order and it should be there in about forty minutes. I will let you go so you can enjoy your meal and get some rest. You have my number, so call if you need anything."

I did not want Gabe to have to worry about cooking or waiting for delivery, so I carefully looked up items that I thought would reheat well. I ordered, what I hoped, would be enough to last him for a few days. If he gives me grief, I will tell him that is why I could not use the gift card on just myself and, really, wouldn't it be a shame for all that money to have just gone to waste?

CHAPTER THIRTEEN

To: Forfriendship33@gmail.com

"Good Morning, Ray. I had to look back through our messages to see if I had mentioned that I was staying at this house with a small army. Ha ha. Again, it is very much appreciated. I can promise you that not a morsel of it will go to waste. I must ask though, who gave you that gift card? Bill Gates? There must have been a pretty penny left on it."

To: 48a813ac33510zch4u@reply.craigslist.org

"Gabe, you are still a growing boy. I wasn't sure what you liked, so I ordered an assortment. In case I have not mentioned it before, I am very glad we have met; virtually at least. You are the first person I have been able to talk to, like this, since Sara. Honestly, with the way the world is today, there are many days I do not even feel like getting out of bed. However, I always look forward to talking to you. Thank you for that. If I still believed in fate, I would think it was fate that led me to your post.

To: Forfriendship33@gmail.com

"My conversations with you are the highlight of my day as well. And yes, the state of the world does seem pretty bad, but you cannot let that get you down. Times have been worse. Times have been better; they have a way of working themselves back around. You don't believe in fate? I find that hard to believe. You said you used to; I am pretty sure I know the answer to this, but why do you not believe in it anymore?"

To: 48a813ac33510zch4u@reply.craigslist.org

"As you said, I am sure you do know the answer, but I stopped believing in fate the day Sara died. I always felt her and I were destined to meet. In fact, we

FATE IS NEVER LATE

joked about it so much that we agreed our first daughter would be named Destiny. We were sixteen. I had left my friend's house late and had to haul ass home to get there by curfew. I walked in twenty minutes late and was prepared for the lecture that I was sure to get. Instead, my mother asked me if I could run back out to the store to get her some cortisone cream. She was making herself a late-night snack and burnt her hand on the toaster oven. Relieved to have dodged the lecture, I headed back out to the store. The parking lot was empty at that time of the night, as you can imagine. Even so, I never park closest to the front door in case there is someone who needs the spot more than I do. I began to pull into a spot about five spaces down when someone, coming from the other lane, began to pull into the same spot. My first thought was, 'Really? With all of these spaces?', but, when I looked, the poor girl's eyes were as big as saucers. We didn't hit each other, but the close call obviously scared her. I held up my hand and backed out of the space. I pulled into a space two slots down. At sixteen, I was not familiar with the layout of the Publix, but I was smart enough to ask an employee where I could find the cream. She told me that I could find it in either of two locations: the pharmacy or the healthcare isle. The pharmacy was too obvious of a choice, and I was really enjoying being out past curfew (don't judge me that my mother was waiting at home with a burn; I was sixteen), so I chose the healthcare isle. As I rounded the corner of the isle, I literally ran into the girl. The package she was carrying, a tube of cortisone cream, fell to the floor. She and I both bent to pick it up and ended up bumping heads. We both laughed, even though it hurt. I told her that I hoped whatever she was buying would help with the bump that she was sure to have on her head now. She said that it wouldn't and showed me her hand. She had a burn about three inches long. 'Pulling slices at work', she explained. I told her my mother had just burned herself as well and that I was there to buy some cortisone cream too. She frowned and told me it was the last tube on the shelf. Using my newfound knowledge of Publix, I told her it was okay that they also had some in the pharmacy. Yes, she looked impressed. She offered to walk with me 'to make sure they did have more'. We began to talk. The conversation continued, in the parking lot, until thirty minutes after the store had closed. When I saw the time, I freaked out. Not only was my mother waiting for me, but it was way after curfew. I wasn't sure if she would be more worried or pissed. Before I left, we exchanged numbers. When I got home, my mother was, again, surprisingly calm. In fact, she was looking at me with a strange smile on her face. When I asked her what the look was for, she told me, 'You look happy.' I gave her the cream, went into my room and called the number listed on the paper, under the name Sara (with a heart). Sara and I talked for hours that night and every day after. We talked every day from the day we met until the day she died. My mother never let me drive that late at night, but that night she needed me to. Had she not got burned, I would never been at that Publix that night. Had Sara not got burned, she would not have been at that Publix that night. It seemed like fate. Yet, if I am to believe that we were destined to meet, I would have to believe that she was destined to die. I am sorry, but I just can't wrap my head around that. With all you have been through, do you believe in fate?"

To: Forfriendship33@gmail.com

"That is completely understandable. What a remarkable story. Thank you so much for sharing that with me. I could picture it all so vividly. Yes, I do believe in fate. I think the problem is that you are looking at everything as happening by fate. However, if that were the case, could you image how people would go through life? They would just be sitting around waiting for fate to happen. I'm

183 | P a g e

pretty sure fate is not available via Amazon Prime. The way I see it, fate is this grand gift from God. It is something He gives to His children simply because He loves them. One thing in your life may be fated-or many. So, He gives you fate, but He also gives you Free Will. Free Will allows you to make an infinite number of choices. Each of these choices will determine the next. Some are complex choices, such as buying a home or applying for a job; others are as simple as two or three sugars in your coffee. Whatever is fated will still find you among all the choices you make. Does that make sense?"

To:48a813ac33510zch4u@reply.craigslist.org

"Yes, that does make sense. So, fate brought us together, but Free Will took her from me? Since God gave us both, I'm sure I can still find some justification in blaming it on Him, but I also understand what you said about Free Will; without it, we would just be actors in a play. What if Free Will would

FATE IS NEVER LATE

have taken Sara before fate intervened? Then I would have just gone through life alone?"

To: Forfriendship33@gmail.com

"I believe that we are all born and die on God's time. I have heard it said before that when we are born, we have an invisible expiration date upon us. As far as the human body is concerned, I feel that is true. Since God sets these times, He will have fate intervene between those times. Don't confuse fate with love. I am not saying we are all fated to fall in love, but we are fated for something. That thing varies from person to person."

To: 48a813ac33510zch4u@reply.craigslist.org

"So, I should be thankful that fate brought me the love of my life; I guess. What about babies that do not make it to delivery or those that pass young? How can they have a fate? I'm sorry if this is too intense; it is a sensitive subject for me."

To: Forfriendship33@gmail.com

"There is no need to apologize. It sounds like this is something you have kept inside. I am happy you feel comfortable enough to talk to me about it. Again, fate has infinite possibilities. Let me begin, first, with babies that do not make it to delivery. God gives us each a soul, at the moment of conception. He chooses the right soul which must be born at the right time. Since free will changes events constantly, the need for the soul to be born, at that particular time, changes. This changes the timeline for that soul. I know what you are going to say, 'How can He devastate parents like that?' I also believe nothing pains God more than having to recall a soul. However, I also believe that He does not take this soul's presence from the parents. At some point in their lives, that soul will touch them again. As for those taken young, have you ever had a moment where one kiss or one look or even one hug has completely changed your life? Something so simple, but it may have been the most important thing in your life; the thing that made you the happiest. If something like that can happen in a moment, then time is irrelevant. As much as we focus on time, we often fail to realize that everything can change in one second; for the better or the worse. I know that you and I realize that, but many people do not. That is why it is so sad when some choose to end their lives. The second after they have done so could have been the second that changed everything for the better. The second they did so, is the second that changed everything for those left behind."

To: 48a813ac33510zch4u@reply.craigslist.org

"Thank you for sharing your thoughts on that. It makes me too sad to keep talking about it, but I think your words hold much wisdom. You should have been a public speaker. Since you brought up suicide, what do you think about it? Do you think it is an unforgivable sin? This is the last depressing topic; I promise. I do not want us to go to sleep with this having been the last thing we discussed."

To: Forfriendship33@gmail.com

"A public speaker, huh? The problem with that is that people need to want to hear what you have to say. No, I do not think suicide is a sin. I believe it comes under the purview of Free Will. If Free Will allows us the ability to make decisions as to what we do in life, it would only make sense that ending said life would be one of those choices. This is such a complex topic. Maybe if someone takes their life before fate has intervened, their soul is returned to earth at some point. Who knows? How can we even guess? I guess the long and short of it is that I do not believe suicide is a sin. So, that being said, what do you think about those Buccaneers?"

To:48a813ac33510zch4u@reply.craigslist.org

"The Buccaneers? Hey, I thought that suicide was going to be our last depressing topic of the night. LOL. Actually, speaking of, I better get to bed; I have an early morning. Good night, sweet dreams and we shall talk again tomorrow.

CHAPTER FOURTEEN

Devin and Destiny were able to come home for a couple days during spring break. Donovan was going to come as well, but his professor picked two students to accompany him to the Adrienne Arsht Center in Miami, for some type of public relations event, and Donovan was one of them. I was very happy for him, but missed him dearly.

On their second day home, Destiny offered to make dinner. She wanted me to invite Vincent and Alan. That sounded nice. Of course, I worried about what might come out of Alan's mouth, but I knew he could refrain from leaking any information with a stern warning. True to her word, Destiny made an amazing dinner which consisted of alfredo pasta with grilled chicken, asparagus with a horseradish drizzle and an avocado and onion enriched salad. She called it that- not me.

FATE IS NEVER LATE

Once I set eyes on the meal, I was impressed but very skeptical. "Where did you learn to cook like this?", I asked her. She could not hide the blush as she turned away. "From watching you, of course.", she replied. I had cooked thousands of meals for this child before. Her only contribution was putting water in a pan- and cold water at that.

"Destiny, remember when you went on that destructive phase when you were little, after having watched 'Drop Dead Fred' and you blamed everything you did on him? Remember how I pretended to believe you? Well, you are no longer eight and I'm no longer buying what you have to sell. How did you go from having to Google how to boil water to creating a meal like this?"

"I told you….", she began.

"Her boyfriend's mother is a chef and she has taught her to cook a lot of things.", Devin blurted, walking into the kitchen.

"Devin!", Destiny yelled.

My head began to spin. A boyfriend? I momentarily wished I had taken a sip of my drink, so I could have dramatically spit it out. This type of information warranted that type of reaction.

"You have a boyfriend?", I asked, "And you have had one long enough that his mother is teaching you to cook?", I continued without pausing for an answer. "Wait. That means you spend time at this mysterious boyfriend's home, as I know damn well your dorm room does not have a kitchen. Are you ever there when his mother is not home?"

Destiny went to answer, but I stopped her. I didn't want to know. God Help Me! "But Daaaaaaaad.", she whined. "Destiny, I do not think I am in the right mindset to handle this right now. Can we talk about it later?"

"My juicy sensor just went off and my juicy sensor is never wrong.", Alan said, walking into the kitchen.

"Don't make me kill you.", I told him. Instead of being offended, he smiled. "Destiny, can you help me get some stuff out of the car?", he asked.

As soon as they left the kitchen, Vincent said, "You know he is only taking her out there to get the gossip, right?"

I picked up the nearest knife. Sure, it was just a paring knife, but it had a blade. "How much do you love him?", I asked Vincent.

"Enough not to have killed him yet or to want to clean up his blood.", he replied.

"Ugh.", I huffed, setting the knife back down, but recalling where it was for future reference. "Destiny has a boyfriend.", I told Vincent.

"And you are upset because you don't?", he laughed.

"Now I see why you and Alan get along so well.", I told him.

"Look, I am not a parent, but I do know how you feel. If I had a daughter, I would castrate any boy who came near her."

"Yes!", I said, throwing up my hands, "So you will help me?"

Vincent laughed. "I love you," he replied, "but I'm not sure if I twenty-five to life love you."

"Alan would help me.", I stated.

Vincent laughed, but his face was not in it. "You are right. He would.", he replied, "So, please don't bring it up to him. I don't have the bail money and he would be on board just for the booking selfie."

I couldn't help but laugh, just picturing Alan in the booking photo. "Okay. You do not have to help me castrate him, but I am not giving you an out on helping me hide the body."

"Deal.", he replied.

When Alan and Destiny came back in, Alan had a shit-eating smirk on his face. It did not escape me that Destiny hung behind him. Great, now these two were chummy! That is all I needed.

"If you say one word, Vincent has given me permission to kill you and has even offered to help me dispose of your body.", I told him.

"Not his body!", Vincent exclaimed, "Destiny's boyfriend's"

"Dad!", Destiny gasped.

"It's not like I have the dumpsite picked out. It's still in the planning stages.", I told her.

She stormed out of the room and we all laughed. "That girl has been very supportive of you. You need to give her the same respect.", Alan said.

Where was that knife? "You are outside with her for ten minutes and you come back in Confucius incarnate?", I said. "First, Confucius has nothing on me. My fashion sense, alone, puts him to shame. Secondly, you know I am right." The shit of it is, I did know he was right.

"I know. I know. It just caught me off guard.", I admitted. "I just don't understand why she wouldn't tell me. We tell each other everything."

Alan rolled his eyes. "Yeah, like you told her about you being gay. Did you tell her about Jake and Justin too?"

I made a mental note to find a dumpsite large enough for two bodies. "There was never any reason to tell her about me being gay. And I'm not gay, I'm more pansexual. And, no, I'm not going to share the details of my love life with my kid."

"Gay, pansexual, bi….they are all variations of the same fact- you like guys. As for her not telling you, maybe she thought, 'I'm not going to share the details of my love life with my dad.'"

I pulled out the barstool to sit down. Alan was right and people were, very likely, ice skating in hell. "You are right.", I said, "I will talk to her tonight."

Alan scooted his barstool closer. "Can you please repeat that?", he asked.

"I said I will talk to her about it tonight.", I said.

"No, darling, the part about me being right."

I looked at Vincent and then to the knife. Vincent just smiled and shook his head.

I went into the room to get Destiny and Devin. "Destiny, I am sorry. It just caught me off-guard. We will talk about it later, okay?", I asked her. She smiled and took my hand.

Devin was about to add his two cents in, but I stopped him in his tracks. "And you boy. You knew about this and just now told me. You had two options: you should have told me about it sooner or you should have kept having you sister's back and not sold her out. You did neither. You and I will be having a little talk later as well." That took the smirk off his face.

Dinner was going great. After sending her my condolences, I would have to compliment Destiny's ex's mother on her cooking skills. Looking around the table brought a huge smile to my face. There were only two people missing that would make it perfect: Donovan and Gabe. No sooner I thought that, the doorbell rang. My heart raced wondering if it could really be one of them. When I opened the door, my heart stopped.

"Hey, daddy.", Jake said.

I pushed him back from the doorway and shut the door. "What the fuck are you doing here?", I asked.

"Whoa. I like it rough, but I did not expect it to begin before we even got inside.", he smirked.

Make that a hole big enough for three! "Jake, what the fuck are you doing here?", I asked again.

"I wanted to see you. I thought you would be happy to see me.", he said. "Well, you though wrong. When I did ever give you the impression that you could just show up at my door?", I asked him.

He did that damn half-smirk. "When you brought me to your place and had your way with me.", he replied.

Was this kid fucking serious? "What the fuck are you; a vampire? Bringing you here once is not a standing invitation. Have you ever heard of a phone?"

Jake was unphased. "I was being spontaneous, you know, like we were that night.", he said, moving forward to kiss me.

I pushed him back again. "Jake, not only is your showing up here extremely inappropriate, my kids are inside. I have guests."

Jake reached out and took my hand. "Well, when you are done playing daddy, give me a call. We can play our own version."

I couldn't decide if I was more pissed or disgusted. "Jake, you need to leave and do not come back. I'm sorry if it was a slow night for you on Grindr, but I am not the answer."

That pissed him off. "Honey, there is no such thing as a slow night for me on Grindr. You should feel privileged that I was giving you a second go at this.", he said, swiping his hands over his body.

"Gee, thank you so much for the privilege, Jake, but, rest assured, I will not be upset, in the least, if you revoke those privileges. In fact, consider them preemptively revoked. You need to leave. Now!", I demanded.

"Your loss.", he said, smiling. If he would have shaken his ass anymore, as he walked away, he would have given himself shaken-twenty-something-syndrome. That may not be a thing, but, right now, I was really wishing it was.

As if I could not be more mortified, when I turned around, everyone had their face pressed to the dining room window. Fuck!

I heard their chairs scrape against the floor as they rushed back to their seats as I entered. They had the audacity to pretend to be eating when I walked into the dining room.

"Do you really think I am blind? Do you really think I did not see all of you watching through the window?", I asked.

"After seeing that guy, I definitely do not think you are blind.", Destiny said. Alan almost choked on his laugh.

"Since you all saw everything, there is no reason to lie. Watch how this works, Destiny. Full disclosure. That was Jake. He and I had a one-night stand awhile back. I have not seen him since and I, definitely, did not expect to see him again."

"Oh. My. God. That was Jake?", Alan said, "You may not be blind, but I question your sanity sending that boy away."

Vincent smacked him. I would have to remember to thank him for that later. "Looks are not everything, Alan.", I shot back, "If you don't believe me, ask Vincent." I know it was a cheesy insult, but it made me feel better.

"Girl, I got the looks, the style and the smarts. Vincent got the whole package when he got me. And speaking of packages."

I cut him off quickly. "Alright. Alright. Enough about Jake. Can we just get back to eating?"

"We can, but the main course just drove away.", Alan said.

I opened my mouth to respond, but Vincent beat me to it. "So, Devin, how is school going?"

Devin stood and pushed his chair back. "Great. Just great.", he huffed, "You know what is also great? You and your father sleeping with the same guy!"

All our mouths dropped as he left the table and headed for his room.

CHAPTER FIFTEEN

"What the…", Alan began.

"Fuck!", I finished for him.

"We really need to come here for dinner more often!", Alan exclaimed.

"Actually, I think that may be our cue to leave.", Vincent said.

"Are you all sure?", I asked, "For all you know, Donovan will show up, at any moment, and announce that he and his professor are engaged."

Alan turned to me. "Is that really a possibility?", he asked.

Vincent grabbed his arm and lifted him. "Let's go, Confucius.", he said.

After seeing them out, I asked Destiny to follow me into Devin's room. "It seems we all have a lot of things we need to discuss. If it is okay with the two of you, I would like for us to discuss

205 | P a g e

then as a family." Both of them nodded.
"I will begin.", I offered.

"I do not have to tell the two of you that losing your mother was unbearable. We did not just lose a wife and a mother, we all lost part of ourselves that night.

However, life can be cruel in many ways. Not only was she taken from us, but we were expected to just continue living with this huge hole that was left in our lives. I don't know if it is the same for the two of you, but I feel like I was thrown out of a shelter and into the storm. The elements are smashing against me and, somehow, I am supposed to fight back when, most of the time, all I want is to let the storm blow me away.

The only thing that keeps me fighting is the two of you and your brother. The three of you are my shelter in the storm. However, day in and day out, I have the lightning crashing around me and I have to do my best to dodge it. I

206 | P a g e

can only imagine it is the same for the three of you; if not worse. I do not want you to feel you have to weather the storm alone. We are all in this together."

"Destiny, I will start with you, as it seems like my situation and Devin's may be a little more complex. As your father, knowing you have a boyfriend is a scary thing. However, I know what a strong woman you are; you are very much your mother's daughter. If you like this boy, he must be something very special. I would very much like to meet him. Am I extremely jealous that his family gets to spend time with you? Definitely! However, that is on me- not you. All that said, if you need me to take you to get on the pill or stock up on condoms, we will go first thing in the morning."

"Dad, if it gives you peace of mind, I am on the pill. I have been for a couple

FATE IS NEVER LATE

years. Donovan took me. It was not too long after mom passed. The stress was wreaking havoc on my periods and Donovan took me to get it checked out. While I was there, they put me on the pill to regulate me. Don't worry, I was not having sex. Seth was my first and we are very safe."

It took a minute for the room to stop spinning. "I am sorry I was not the one to take you. Please know, if you ever need anything, I am here. So, Seth huh?"

Destiny smiled.

"Devin. This is awkward, to say the least. Of course, not that you are gay, although, I wish you would have felt comfortable enough to tell me. We apparently have this...situation... with Jake to discuss. I want you to know that it was not something I planned. It was a one-time thing that resulted from a night when I was very lost, lonely and confused. I did not invite him over tonight. In fact, I have not seen or spoken to him since that one night. How do you know him?"

"Jake is Jack's older brother.", Devin replied.

"Your best friend, Jack?", I asked to clarify.

"Yes, that Jack."

"Oh my God, Devin. That makes all of this so much weirder, if that is possible. How did that come about?", I asked.

"First, dad, I want you to know that I never felt uncomfortable letting you know I am gay. Honestly, and I feel bad even saying this, but I was more worried about how mom would take it. I don't know how to explain it. I always suspected she knew, but she would always ask me if I had a girlfriend. And you know she was always trying to set me up with this or that girl. I don't know. I just felt that she knew but did not want to know."

"Oh Devin, I am sorry you felt that way. I think that may have more to do with me than it did with you. You see, your mother knew I dated men before her and I got together. I think, maybe in the back of her mind, that always bothered her. Of course, she never had any reason for it to, but that is not how the mind works sometimes."

"I understand.", Devin replied, "I would have told you both eventually, but I was going to wait until I had a steady boyfriend before doing so."

I pulled him in for a hug and Destiny joined in. "So, this thing you had with Jake, it wasn't serious?"

Devin wiped a tear from his eye. "Not for him. I had a crush on him for years. I always tried my best to not look at him when he was around. However, there were many times he would catch me looking at him and he would just smile. When I was a freshman, he was a senior, so I would see him around school more often.

I had heard rumors that he may be gay, but I also heard that Amy Mastersen gave birth to triplets in the girl's bathroom. You know how high school is. One night, toward the end of his senior year, I was sleeping over at Jack's. I got up in the middle of the night to get a drink of water and Jake was just getting home. I tried to hurry back to Jack's room, but he told me I didn't have to rush off. He asked me how I liked school and we began to talking.

I was so nervous and he noticed. He grabbed ahold of my hand and asked why I was so nervous. I tried to make up some lie, but before I could get it out, he kissed me. One thing led to another and...well...that is how Jake became my first. Of course, after that, he acted like it had never happened."

I pulled Devin in for another hug. "I am so sorry your first experience was like that. Especially with someone you had a crush on for so long. You do know that Jake is a prick and you deserve so much better than him, right?"

Devin smiled. "So do you.", he laughed.

"You know what, kid? We are both right. So how about we don't give Jake any more credit than he is worth. He is a mistake we both made and nothing more."

"Well, this may not be a good time to tell you all.", Destiny said. Devin and I both looked at her with our jaw on the ground. "I am just kidding!", she laughed, "I have so much better taste than the two of you."

We both grabbed a pillow and began pelting Destiny with them.

When we finally settled down, we agreed that there would be no more secrets between us. "What about Donovan?", I asked them, "Any major revelations I need to know about him?" Destiny and Devin gave each other that look. "Oh shit. What?", I asked. They both started laughing. I picked the pillows back up and the pillow fight started all over again.

Once I was settled in for the night, I messaged Gabe.

To:48a813ac33510zch4u@reply.craigslist.org

"Gabe, I hope you had an amazing day. My day was beyond interesting. I don't think I can relive it all at this moment, but I will tell you all about it tomorrow. You have my cell number, call if you need anything. Good night."

CHAPTER SIXTEEN

I woke up to sixteen text messages from Alan and an email from Gabe. I needed caffeine before I could focus on either of them; especially the texts.

After my second cup of coffee, I began with the text, to get them out of the way. Of course, all the texts consisted of asking what else "juicy" happened after he left. I knew it would drive him nuts, so all I replied was, "I will tell you later." I then opened my email.

To: Forfriendship33@gmail.com

"Beyond interesting, huh? I would be lying if I did not say you have me intrigued. I leave you alone for one day….. Haha."

I sent Gabe a reply summarizing everything that happened the night before. I laughed when I envisioned the emotional skidmark it would leave him with. I am surprised that Gabe still speaks to me. I messaged him to try to make his life easier; instead, I drag him into the craziness, that is my life, every day. Who knows, maybe my disfunction makes him feel a little better about his own life?

I didn't wait for a reply. I knew it would take him awhile to read the small novel I sent him and I had to take the kids back to school today. I looked forward to seeing his reply when I arrived back at home.

I hoped to see Donovan, when I dropped the kids off, but he was not yet back from his trip to Miami. We agreed that we would let Donovan hear about the events from the weekend from whomever he chose.

I sent him a text letting him know that his siblings were safely back at school. I warned him that the weekend was a little crazy and told him that I would be happy to fill him in on what happened, or he could ask his brother and sister.

I did not want him to feel like I was hiding anything from him. If there was one thing I learned this weekend, it was that you could tuck something out of sight, but that does not mean it will stay hidden.

I had a couple hours drive home, so I figured I would get the inevitable over with; I called Alan. I swear I could hear the boy salivating over the phone. He suggested that I sleep with Seth, so the kids did not feel like I was playing favorites.

In turn, I suggested he go fuck himself. When he replied, "Funny you should say

FATE IS NEVER LATE

that." I hung up! I pulled up Audible and put on "Legend of the Loa". Maybe listening to Gris' family drama would take my mind off of my own.

The drive home this time was so different than the first time. It was a chaotic but great weekend. This time, there was a smile on my face. It seems like so much went wrong, yet so much went right.

Gabe would appreciate how so many random events culminated this weekend. Normally the events would have had me out of my mind with worry. Strangely, I was at peace.

To: Forfriendship33@gmail.com

"Ray, at the center of all chaos is peace determined to break through. It sounds to me as through peace prevailed. Am I wrong? I know it cannot be easy knowing your baby girl has a man in her life. I have no doubts that you raised a very smart, very strong girl. She is her daddy's daughter; she will be fine. Have you made plans to meet the boy yet? I am sure you will feel better once you have.

As for what happened with Devin, what are the chances that the stranger you met at the bar that night would be your son's childhood crush? After so much time, what are the chances that Jake would show up at your door that night? You now know that the burden and worry you have carried inside you has been carried by Devin as well. A burden, when shared, begets bonding.

You may thing me crazy, but I am very happy for you; all of you."

To:48a813ac33510zch4u@reply.craigslist.org

"Gabe, peace very much prevailed. Today, I am happy. It has been a very long time since I could say that. In fact, I had not realized how much I was just phoning it in. I convinced myself that existing was the same as happiness. With that revelation came others. My happiness has always come from others; being with them, taking care of them. I never had the need to stop and ask myself if I was actually happy with me. It is really a mind-blowing question. It has never been just me. I have no idea who I am beyond being a husband and a father. It is time I find out. I cannot be part of something 'more' until I discover the pieces that make me whole within. Does that make sense?"

To: Forfriendship33@gmail.com

"Ray, it makes perfect sense. I pray you come to see in yourself what others see in you; what I see in you. One final piece of advice, do not alienate yourself in your quest. Finding yourself does not equate to being by yourself. Sometimes the best way to discover who you are is by seeing it through the eyes of others. Find whatever makes you happy and do it. Once you have found that, you can then figure out how that intertwines with everything else. Everything and everyone is part of it all. It's not necessarily who you may need, it very well may be who needs you. Sometimes the piece of ourselves, which we give to others, is the piece that completes us. And Ray, I also believe that when Free Will engages with fate, fate is not lost forever; it is released back into the universe, patiently waiting for its time to come. One thing I believe we have both learned is that fate is never late."

CHAPTER SEVENTEEN

I was so in awe by his message, that it was not until I reread it that his words, "One final piece of advice" struck me. Something about the way he phrased it gave me an uneasy feeling. I replied to Gabe, but no reply came. Not that night. Not the next day. Not a week later. The weeks turned into a month. "One final piece of advice." That is all that ran through my mind. I feared the worst. I had to know.

"Hey Vincent, it's me. Can you do me a favor?", I asked.

"As long as it does not involve manual labor or anything gynecological, you know I am your man.", he replied.

"I need you to track down the owner of an email address for me."

Vincent snickered. "Am I risking jail time for this? You are not stalking tall, dark and potentially married from Starbucks, are you?", he asked.

"No.", I laughed, wondering why I never asked him to do that for me, "Just an old friend."

"Hmmmm. If he is such an old friend, why don't you know this information?", he teased.

I was glad he could not see my shot him a bird through the phone. "Vincent, are you going to hook a brother up or not?", I asked. Silence. "Vincent?", I asked, staring at the phone, like I could somehow see him through the device. "I'm here. I just wanted to make you sweat.", he said, "You shot me a bird, didn't you?"

I looked at the phone again, just to make sure that I didn't accidentally Facetime him. "You just looked at your phone to make sure you didn't Facetime me, didn't you?", he asked.

"Remind me why we are friends.", I replied.

"Because you love me and because no one else has the insane IT skills that I have to track down your mystery email lover.", he replied.

"First of all, it is not a lover. Secondly, who ever said it was a man. Assume much?", I asked.

"Because the only women you would have me track down are Dolly Pardon or Tootie from Facts of Life and we both know that tracking down either may be too much for even my advanced skills.", he replied.

"Touche.", I replied, "It is a man, but it is not like that. We have been emailing back and forth for a while now and I just want to know a little more about him."

"Have you thought to ask him?", he replied.

"Wow, Vincent, what a great idea. You could put Dr. Phil and Oprah out of a job with that type of insight and wisdom.", I huffed.

"Hey, no talking about Oprah. You know I worship at the shrine of O every night before bed."

"Yeah, that is because that is the only O you are going to have before you go to bed.", I shot back.

"Sorry, did the line go dead?", he asked.

"Alright, I am sorry.", I said.

"Say it.", he replied.

"Must I?", I asked.

"You know you must."

I rolled my eyes and sighed into the phone. "You know that Oprah can see if you rolled your eyes right?", he said. "Seriously, can you see me through my camera or something?", I asked.

"Maybe. Now say it!", he demanded. "Oprah is the queen of all she surveys. We shall bow before her wisdom and beauty.", I said, reluctantly.

"Finish it.", he said.

"Oh hell no. I will concede to your worship of Oprah, but I only say Amen when speaking to or about one person. You know that."

"Alright, I guess that is sufficient.", he replied.

"So, are you going to help me?", I asked.

"What were you calling about again?", he asked.

"Vincent!", I practically yelled into the phone.

"That is right.", he said, "You want me to give you information on this person who may or may not be your lover, but is definitely not Dolly or Tootie."

Before I could vocalize my growing frustration, he added, "What is the email address."

"Don't kill me, but it is the email assigned by Craigslist. I don't have an actual email address for him.", I confessed.

"Are you kidding me?", he replied, "How about I just track down Dolly instead?"

I gripped the phone in my palm, hoping somehow the crushing vibrations would travel through the line. "Are you telling me that is above your level of expertise?", I asked, knowing the verbal jab at his skills would hurt him worse than the virtually pain I was trying to inflict through the phone.

"I didn't say that.", he replied, "I was just reflecting on the irony that you could have posted an ad on Craigslist for someone to help you with this and, for all you know, it could have been your mystery man that replied. Imagine the laugh the two of you could have had over that."

"I could also inquire on Craigslist to find a hitman. You are aware of this, right?", I replied.

"Okay. Okay. What is the email address?", he finally asked.

"It is 48a813ac33510zch4u@reply.craigslist.org", I read off, to make sure I gave it to him correctly.

"Could it be any longer?", he asked.

"I didn't create the email address. Shall I contact Craig and pass along your displeasure to him?"

"That would be great. Tell him that I am a big fan of the *Best Of* section. That guy looking for the woman who farted on the subway was priceless."

I contemplated throwing the phone down and jumping on it until it was nothing but tempered glass and bad memories; however, I remembered it was a lease and decided against it.

"I am sure your admiration will make Craig's day. So, how long do you think it will take you to track it down?", I asked.

"About ten seconds ago.", he said, the smile evident in his voice.

"What? You are telling me you already have the information?", I asked, both dumbfounded and in disbelief.

"Did you really have any doubt?", he asked.

"Hell yes, I did.", I blurted, "I have always secretly suspected you ran a porn site for a living."

"I don't run one, but you may come across someone who looks a lot like me; depending on the site of course.", he replied.

"How does Alan put up with you?", I sighed.

"I just keep him fed. You know what they say, 'The way to a man's heart is through his stomach.'"

"Well, the way to this man's heart is by finally giving him the information. What did you find?", I asked.

"It does not provide much information. All I could find was the email address he used to sign up for the Craigslist account.", he replied.

My heart dropped, but at least it was something to go on. "That is better than nothing.", I replied, "What is his email address?"

"It is Forfriendship33@gmail.com.", he said.

I shook my head. I didn't want to let him know that was mine, but I needed him to investigate it further. "That can't be it. Can you check again?", I asked him.

"First you doubt Oprah and now you doubt me?", he said, "I do believe my heart is broken."

"Vincent, seriously, can you please check again? There has to be another email address associated with the account.", I told him.

"No, sir. I can tell you with 100 percent certainty that is the email address that was used to sign up for the account."

Something was wrong. Perhaps Craigslist only embedded the email address of the original sender into the reply address. I would have to research this on my own.

"Thank you. I will take that information and look into it a little more on my end.", I said.

"Did that help?", he asked.

"Yes, thank you. That helps a lot.", I lied.

FATE IS NEVER LATE

"I'm glad I could help.", he said, "Oh, about what we were talking about earlier... you know, the porn site...I would not advise you to look up menwithsheep.com."

I could hear him laughing as I hit end call.

After thirty or so Google searches, I finally found a link where, alleged, hackers were talking about tracing email addresses for Craigslist accounts. The information contained in their thread left me as confused as when I began the search.

According to their back-and-forth, the address used to send a reply in Craigslist could in fact be hacked to trace the primary email address used to set up the account. It was a measure put in place by Craigslist to cover their ass if need be.

But how could that be? I looked at the email address that Vincent gave me again. Forfriendship33@gmail.com. That was my email address! There was something wrong here.

I pulled out my laptop because some things were not meant to be done on a smartphone. I pulled up my email account and retrieved the email thread between Gabe and me. It took me about forty-five minutes, but I was able to get to the first conversation he and I had.

From there, I worked my way forward. I retrieved pen and paper, so I could write down anything that stood out; anything that may help me track down who Gabe was.

I first wrote down the stuff I knew off the top of my head. Gabe was local; at least within a few counties from me. He was born and raised here and traveled very little during his life. He was married for forty years and had lost his wife to cancer almost six years ago. Maybe I could search local obituaries, around that time frame, which listed a Gabriel as the surviving spouse? I spent the next two hours doing just that. There were twelve possibilities within the five counties closest to me.

The addresses! I would do a reverse search on the addresses he had provided to me when he, reluctantly, allowed me to send him items. It took me another two hours to go through the email thread to find the addresses. After I had them all written down, I began to search each of them in Google. I thought I was confused before I started the search; that was nothing compared to my state of mind after.

The first address, where he had me send the handwritten letter, belonged to a nursing home. Gabe always said he lived alone. Could I have found him as easily as going to the nursing home listed at the first address? I picked up the phone to call them and ask to speak to Gabriel, but I didn't have a last name. What was I going to do, ask to speak to every Gabriel that lived there? Who would I say I was? Maybe that is something better done in person.

The nursing home was only forty minutes from my home. I grabbed my car keys and headed out. I was so excited about the possibly of finally meeting Gabe.

Excited and nervous. I reached down, to the cupholder, to grab a cigar and smiled as my hand came up empty. Thanks to Gabe, I had not smoked in weeks. How awful would that have been, anyway, to show up smelling of smoke when he lost his wife to lung cancer.

My heart dropped as I pulled into the parking lot of the nursing home. There were a couple of people sitting in wheelchairs, oxygen tanks strapped to their back, scattered around the property. Their pale gowns barely covering their even paler and withered legs.

Where were the orderlies, I wondered? Of course, it was not like these people were going to run off. If they were here, they probably had no other place they could go.

I was met with blank stares as I said 'hello' to those I passed. When I reached the front desk, the young lady behind the counter plastered on the best fake smile she could muster.

"Hello. How may I help you?", she asked.

If her day was trying, I was not about to make it any easier. "I know this is going to sound weird, but I am looking for a man named Gabriel.", I told her.

She inhaled and held the breath.

"What is Gabriel's last name?", she asked, turning to her computer screen. "Well, that is the weird part.", I told her, "I do not know his last name."

She rubbed the palm of her hand over her right eye. "What is your relationship to the patient?", she asked.

"I am a friend.", I stammered.

Her head remained still but her eyes looked up at me. "And you do not know your friend's last name?", she said, exhaling heavily.

"We met online.", I told her, quickly adding, "We were both in need of someone to talk to and we began emailing back and forth. I can show you the emails if you like."

She looked at me with pity in her eyes. "No, sir, that is alright. However, without a last name, I am afraid I cannot be of much help to you."

I expected as much, but it still sucked to hear her say it.

"Do you work here often?", I asked her. Now she was looking at me like I was using a cheesy pick-up line on her. "I only ask because I mailed him a letter. If you are normally on shift, perhaps you remember it. He had me address it to 'My New Friend' at this address. I know all of this sounds weird, but I thought I was sending it to him directly."

"Yes!", she exclaimed, "I remember that letter." My heartbeat increased to match my excitement. "Since it did not have a recipients name, we hung it on the bulletin board over there.", she said, pointing to the elementary-like framed board on the wall.

237 | P a g e

"We were hoping one of the residents would recognize it and claim it.", she said, "Unfortunately, none of them did." My heart sank again.

"What happened to the letter?", I asked. "We gave it to one of our residents, Mary. You see, Mary had been here for seven years or so; well before I started here. She was suffering from dementia. Poor thing had no family. I guess that was for the best, as she would not have remembered them from one moment to the next. Anyway, although she had dementia, she's smart as a whip. She could recite 'David Copperfield' from memory, but could not recall where she originally read it. Eighty-seven years old and still had her real teeth. Never needed glasses a day in her life."

"Mary loved to read. She would read anything we gave to her. Of course, we had to give her short stories, as she would forget what she had read and would start again from the beginning. One day, Mary asked me if I had heard from her family. It broke my heart. The entire time I have worked here, Mary has never had a visitor. Since your letter was sitting unclaimed, I gave it to her and told her that it was from her family. She had a smile on her face the entire time she read it. Having forgotten she had already read it, she must have read it twenty more times that day. Mary died that very night. When we found her, she had the letter snuggled against her heart; she still had a smile on her face."

I could not stop the tears that fell; nor would I have wanted to. The woman embraced me. "I am so sorry.", she said. I did not bother to wipe the tears from my face. "There is nothing to be sorry for.", I replied, "Thank you very much for what you did. Gabriel told me that the letter brought a never-ending smile. I just assumed it was he that was smiling."

FATE IS NEVER LATE

The lady, Kimberly I learned, hugged me again. "If there is any other information you can give me, I will do what I can to help you find Gabriel.", she offered.

"Thank you. I am not sure if Gabriel was ever here, but I do not believe he is here now." I thanked her again and left.

All the way home, the smile never left my face. I was not sure why Gabriel would not have claimed the letter, but I am glad it went to someone who needed it. He must have been there; how else would he have known it brought a never-ending smile? I couldn't wait to get home to look up the next address.

The second address that Gabe provided to me was the one that supposedly belonged to a man he worked with for many years. The man was going out of town and Gabe offered to take care of his fish and his plants when he was gone. He told me that it would was something he could do, which would not be too taxing on him and would also provide him with enjoyment. He found the fish both entertaining and relaxing, he said. I felt the change of atmosphere may be good for him.

It was to that address that Gabe allowed me to send him some food from DinnerDash. He mentioned he was hungry but felt guilty eating the man's food. I knew he was going to be there for a couple more days, so I sent him enough food to last him, careful to choose items that would not go bad quickly. He thanked me over and over, telling me that it provided much needed nourishment and was the best meal he had since his wife died. I was so happy that something so simple could mean so much to him. Surely, this man he worked with would know where I could find Gabe.

241 | P a g e

I was relieved to find the address belonged to a private residence. Again, the location was no more than a thirty minute drive, so I headed out again.

When I arrived, I had to double check the address. It is not like Gabe provided me with a description of the home, he would never invade someone's privacy that way, but the home was not what I expected.

It was a little white house (that is, what little paint was left on it was white). There was a rusted chain link fence doing what it could to protect the sparse children's toys which were scattered in the yard.

I did not expect his coworker to have children. Gabe gave me the impression the man was around his age and lived alone. Perhaps the toys belonged to his grandchildren.

As I approached the gate, which was barely holding on, a woman opened the door. She wore a pajama gown with stained blue slippers. Her hair was disheveled and it looked like she had not slept for days. Even though her appearance betrayed her, I could tell she was much younger than she appeared. "Can I help you?", she asked.

"Yes ma'am. At least I hope you can. I am looking for a man named Gabriel. I believe he took care of your grandfather's fish and plants awhile back."

I could tell she was distracted, but she fought to not let it show. "I'm sorry, but unless by awhile back, you mean twenty years or so, you have the wrong place. My grandfather passed away in 1998."

I dropped my hand from the latch on the gate. "I am sorry for your loss. Perhaps it was your father?", I asked. She laughed. "Sir, that would be even more of a miracle. My father left before I was even born."

"Again, I am sorry.", I told her.

"Why did you tell him to leave?", she said.

I didn't know what to say.

"I am just messing with you.", she said, "Sorry, but you have the wrong house."

A baby began to cry inside the home. "I'm sorry, I have to go.", she said. "One more thing.", I called out.

She looked inside the home and then back to me.

"Have you lived her for a while?", I asked her.

She took a step backwards, so her body was not inside the house.

FATE IS NEVER LATE

"Look, I indulged your questions, but you really need to leave.", she warned.

"I only ask because I had food delivered to my friend at this address not long ago.", I told her.

The baby continued to cry. "Look, if you want money for the food, I can't help you. I have to go."

"No ma'am, I am not looking for payment, just for my friend.", I called out.

When she walked into the house, I turned to leave. She reappeared at the door with the child in her arms. The child had the unmistakable smile and aura of genuine love that all children with down syndrome possessed.

"The food was delivered here. I told the driver he had the wrong house, but he verified the address. He told me the food was already paid for so either I was to take it or he would have to throw it away; so, I took it. I'm sorry if it was not delivered to the home you intended, but as I said, if you are looking for reimbursement, I cannot help you."

"No. I promise you, I am not looking for money. I was just looking for my friend who I thought was staying at this address at the time. I could have sworn this was the address he gave me.", I told her.

"Does this house look like it has had the attention of a man recently? Hell, do I look like I have had the attention of a man recently?", she asked, then she blushed. "Oh my God. I did not mean it to come out like that.", she said.

I laughed. "I understand what you meant. I am sorry to have bothered you.", I said, turning to leave.

She called out to me. "Hey, if it makes you feel any better, that was the best meal..meals actually..I had in years. I had just gotten home from an extended stay with John in the hospital.", she said, moving her head to indicate the child she was holding.

"Truth be told, I had no food in the house. The hospital took every last dime I had, as a down payment, before they would even treat John. Can you believe those bastards? They would have let him die right there in the waiting room had I not had enough to appease them for the time being. Anyway, that food arrived shortly after we had gotten home. The hospital would only feed John, so I had not had anything more than a granola bar in three days. I considered not even telling the driver he had the wrong house, but karma, you know? I burst into tears when he told me I would need to keep the food or they would throw it away. So, I know it was not meant for me, but thank you anyway.", she said.

I had a feeling the food went exactly where it was meant to go. "You are very welcome.", I said.

Before I pulled away from her home, I pulled up the DinnerDash app, went into my order history and reordered the same items to be delivered to her again. "What is going on, Gabriel?", I asked the air, a smile on my face. It had been a long day, but I couldn't wait to get home to check the third address.

Have you ever driven somewhere and not remembered how you got there? That is how it was when I arrived home. My mind was not only going over the events of the day, I was also wondering if the third address would finally lead me to Gabe.

The third address was not a specific location; nor was it one that Gabe provided to me. It was a general location that I had put together from places Gabe had mentioned over the years.

The diner where he always took his favorite waitress, Stella, some of his homemade cornbread. She always thanked him with a hug, which I still think is the main reason he went there so often.

The coffee shop where the owner, Frank, would always ask him where he has been; telling him that he missed him, even though it had only been a day or two since he was last there.

The flower shop where he always picked up a bunch of dandelions, which was his wife's favorite flower. He always kept some in the vase next to her side of the bed.

I knew it would be a long shot, but since Gabe's condition limited his ability to travel, I googled areas that had a diner, coffee shop and flower shop within close vicinity. The area was in-between the first two addresses, so I felt fairly confident. If nothing else, I would have three places where I could inquire about Gabe.

It was late, so I would set out first thing in the morning. I feel asleep thinking of Mary's smile and hoping the food brought the loving mother a matching smile.

Although I was anxious to begin my day's journey, I made a batch of cornbread to take to Gabe. We always playfully debated whose cornbread was better; I would finally be able to let him decide the victor for himself.

The first place I stopped at was the diner. The staff at diners normally take the time to get to know their customers. With the bond Gabe had with Stella, she was my best bet at getting information. Who knows, maybe I would luck out and Gabe would be there.

No such luck. The woman who greeted me, Ethel, assured me they have never had a waitress by the name of Stella. Although I was disappointed, I could not help but laugh when I realized the name of the diner was "The Last Chance Diner." I only hoped that was not an omen.

Since there was ample parking available, I left my car parked there and walked to the coffee shop. I checked the sign on the window to verify the name was not "Last Chance Coffee." If so, I was going to turn around and leave.

Thankfully, it was not. In fact, the quirky name brought a smile to my face. It was, "Where Have You Bean?" The owner, Brad, informed me they did have a barista by the name of Frank; however, he left for college the day before, which is why he was working the counter.

He informed me that, although he normally works behind the scenes, he knows the regular customers well. He did not know of anyone named Gabe which matched the description. My disappointment was only slightly quelled by the incredible aroma of the fresh roasted beans. Coffee has always been my vice, so I might as well drown my sorrows.

I thanked Brad for the information and ordered a large White Chocolate Mocha. "If you add a slice of banana bread, you get one of our t-shirts for free.", Brad offered.

Why not? I took him up on his offer. As I left, I thanked Brad again and asked him if he could direct me to the florist. Luckily, it was right across the way, on the other side of the park. Having had no luck at the first two locations, I was not holding out much hope, but I was here; might as well check it out.

I decided to walk through the park. I have always loved the fact that someone put their foot down and demanded we keep an area free of development. A plot of land, regardless of how small in comparison, where nature still has a foothold.

A place where you can sit on actual grass and watch the squirrels play their version of tag. A place where you can lean against a tree and get lost in a book while the birds sing to each other from above. To me, a park is God's fingerprint; a place He touched, showing us the beauty of His original design.

Being in no rush to probably get disappointed again, I decided to sit on a bench and enjoy the surroundings. As I watched a brother and sister playing hide and go seek, I was taken by surprise when a dog buried his head in my crotch.

"Whoa, boy, buy me dinner first.", I laughed. That is when I remembered I still had the cornbread in the pocket of my jacket. "Stella! Get over here!", a man yelled, quickly running up to retrieve the dog.

"It's okay.", I assured him, "I have four at home. I know how it is.", I laughed. "I am so sorry.", he said, "Stella normally does not leave my side."

I looked at the dog, whose nose was easily sniffing out the cornbread. "Her name is Stella?", I asked, not believing the coincidence.

"Yes. My girlfriend loves 'A Streetcar Named Desire'. I had no choice in the name." I laughed imagining his futile attempt at picking the dog's name.

"I think she smells the cornbread in my pocket.", I told him.

"That explains it!", he exclaimed, "Stella loves cornbread. My girlfriend, Trish, would bake it all the time when Stella was a puppy. It is the only 'people-food' we allow her to eat."

Knowing the chance of giving it to Gabe was slim-to-none, I figured I may as well let Stella have it. "Would you mind if I gave her some?", I asked him.

"No. Not at all.", he replied, "But before you do, let me show you something."

He asked Stella to sit, which she quickly did, and he had me stand in front of her. "Hold the cornbread in front of you, but tell her 'not yet'.", he said. When you are ready, let her know she can have it."

I held it out and couldn't help but laugh at the eagerness in Stella's eyes. "Okay, girl, you can have it.", I said. Stella quickly, but gingerly, swallowed the cornbread offered.

"Now brace yourself.", he said. Before I could register what he was saying, Stella raised up on her hind legs, placing her front paws on my shoulders. "She thanks you with a hug. I taught her that!", he said proudly.

The tears flowed before I felt them coming. "Oh my God, I am sorry. Did she hurt you?", the man asked.

I hugged Stella back. "No. Not at all. On the contrary; she made my day.", I assured him.

I rubbed Stella's head and asked her to sit. I then offered her another piece or cornbread and laughed and cried as she thanked me with another hug. "She is a great dog.", I told him.

"Well, I think you have a friend for life now.", he replied.

"That works for me.", I told him.

He said they had to leave, so I gave him the remaining cornbread to take home for Stella. I bent down to hug Stella goodbye. "You deserve one too.", I told her.

I stood there in awe watching them walk away. There was no way this was a coincidence. I didn't know what to think, but my soul was soaring. I sat back down to take everything in.

As I was looking around to see if anyone resembled Gabe, I noticed the hot dog stand across the park. I had to put on my glasses to verify I was not misreading the name. It was "Frank's Franks". I leapt up and quickly made my way to the stand.

The first thing I noticed was the vendor's shirt. It was the "Where Have You Bean?" shirt from the coffee shop. "Where have you bean?", the man said. "Excuse me?", I said.

"My shirt; I saw you looking at it. It is from the coffee shop across the way. It says, 'Where Have You Bean'. That is the name of the shop."

"I know.", I laughed, pulling out my shirt. I just came from there.

"And now you have arrived at the best hot dog stand in the country.", he boasted, "What would you like?"

I could not speak. I just looked at him dumbfounded.

"Would you like a suggestion?", he asked.

"I'm sorry.", I told him, "Are you Frank?"

He laughed. "The one and only. I gave the rest of the staff the day off.", he joked.

"You wouldn't happen to know a man named Gabe, would you?", I asked.

"The only Gabe I know is right over there.", he said, pointing at a spot to my left.

I turned quickly, but did not see anyone. "I'm sorry, but where is he?" He laughed again. "Right there. You can't miss him. Biggest statue in the park.", he said.

My heart sank again. "Thank you.", I said, turning to leave.

"You sure there is nothing I can get for you?", he asked.

"No, thank you.", I replied, "I don't think what I am looking for is here."

With my head hanging, I headed back to my car. As I neared the statue, which Frank was telling me about, an overwhelming smell of dandelions hit me.

It can't be; that is Gabe's wife's favorite flower! When I looked for the source of the smell, I saw that the statue was surrounded by the flowers. I approached the flowers and took one in my hand. I pulled a flower to take it with me and that is when I saw the plaque hidden behind it. It said, "Archangel Gabriel: Watch over us always."

My head was spinning and my knees grew weak. I had no choice but to sit on the ground. When the dizziness began to subside, I looked up at the statue. Underneath Gabriel's feet was another plaque. It said, "Never will I leave you or forsake you. Even in your loneliest moment, you are never alone.- Jesus"

I did not try to stop the flow of tears that ran down my cheeks. They were tears of joy; they were tears of hope; they were tears of Faith.

I sat there staring at the statue for at least an hour. Every conversation with Gabe led me here. However, I realized it was not only the destination, but the journey. In trying to help Gabe, he was actually helping me.

My actions took me out of my comfort zone and helped me grow; helped me expand my horizons. In the process, I was able to help others, those who were in desperate need, without even realizing I was doing so.

I always thought I was stuck; taking one step forward and two steps back. Thinking I had no purpose in life anymore; thinking I would forever be alone. All that time, I was moving forward; even though I was not paying attention to the scenery changing.

In two days, I met Kimberly. I met the loving mother, whose name I promised myself I would learn. I met Ethel and Brad. I met Stella and her owner. I met Frank. All people that I would have never spoken to had it not been for my journey to find Gabe.

I realized I was never alone; I was simply not allowing myself to see those who surrounded me.

It was not that I was not connected; we are all connected- I was detached. Maybe I was scared to feel; scared of the hurt I knew it could bring. Yet, I wasn't completely detached.

There was Gabe. I reached out to Gabe and, in return, he reached into me. Piece by piece he removed the doubt;

FATE IS NEVER LATE

he removed the hurt. He led me on a journey where I had no choice but to pay attention to the scenery. In two days, I was able to see so much that I had turned a blind eye to. The best part, I wanted to see more; I wanted to see it all.

As I walked back to my car, my thoughts were no longer on finding Gabe; I knew I had already found him. My next stop would be the toy store to purchase some toys for John. I would deliver them to his mother, along with some groceries. The only thing I would ask for in return was her name. After that, I would head to the nursing home to ask Kimberly if they had any volunteer positions available.

When I arrived at home, I opened my email and hit reply on the now inactive email thread with Gabe. I typed, "Gabe, I know I will not receive a reply to this email and I wanted to let you know that is okay. I am okay. I am more than okay, thanks to you. If you did reply, I believe I know you well enough now to know what you would say. You would say, 'The Lord helps those who help themselves.'

Thank you for guiding me in the process of helping myself; even when I did not feel worthy of the help. Thank you for opening my eyes to others which are in need. And, above all else, thank you for never leaving me."

I closed my laptop and got into bed with a smile on my face. Tomorrow was my first day volunteering at the nursing home. After that, who knows what awaited me. Whatever it was, I would approach it with an open mind and an open heart. And when I got home at the end of the day, I would open my email and tell Gabe all about the adventures of my day.

EPILOGUE

I opened by laptop and went to the bookmark titled, "Craigslist/Tampa/MissedConnections". My intent was to delete it; the only reason I had it there was to view Gabe's original post. However, when I right clicked on the link, instead of giving me the option to delete it, it opened the page.

The first post was titled, "Yesterday at the Park". I laughed out loud. How could I not click on it? The post read:

"I hope this does not sound too stalker-like, but I saw you at the park yesterday. You looked a little sad, but determined. Just as I built up the courage to say hello, you began speaking to a man who was there with his dog. Just when I figured I had lost my chance, you ended your

265 | P a g e

conversation and headed to the hotdog stand.

I didn't know if you saw me and I didn't want you to think I was following you, but I figured buying a hot dog would be innocent enough. Hopefully you would have to wait for yours and that would give us a moment to talk. However, you didn't order; it looked like you were just asking the vendor for directions.

I still went and ordered one (you should have gotten one, it was delicious) because I felt foolish at that point. Once I had my hotdog, I turned to look for you; I was hoping you were still in the park. That is when I saw you by the statue of the Archangel Gabriel. I hope you don't mind me mentioning this on here, but you were crying and it broke my heart. I wanted to run up to you and comfort you, but I did not know how you would feel about that.

FATE IS NEVER LATE

I left with a heavy heart. I would love to meet you, if for nothing else, to make sure you are okay. I believe in fate, so if it is meant to be, somehow you will see this post.- Paul"

I clicked on "Reply". "Paul, I have recently learned that, even if you do not believe in fate, fate believes in us. I will be at the park in an hour. I believe you will be too. Look forward to meeting you.- Ray"

Made in the USA
Columbia, SC
05 April 2023

14409821R00146